D0679535

DISCARDED
from the Nashville Public Library

NO PARKING AT THE END TIMES

BRYAN BLISS

GREENWILLOW BOOKS
An Imprint of HarperCollins*Publishers*

This book is a work of fiction. References to real people, events, establishments, organizations, or locales are intended only to provide a sense of authenticity, and are used to advance the fictional narrative. All other characters, and all incidents and dialogue, are drawn from the author's imagination and are not to be construed as real.

 Printed in the United States of America. For information address HarperCollins Children's Books, a division of HarperCollins Publishers, 195 Broadway, New York, NY 10007.

www.epicreads.com

The text of this book is set in 11-point Sabon.
Book design by Paul Zakris
Library of Congress Cataloging-in-Publication Data

Bliss, Bryan.
No parking at the end times / Bryan Bliss.
"Greenwillow Books."
pages cm
Summary: Abigail's parents, believing the end of the world is near, sell their house, give the money to an end-of-times preacher, and drive from North Carolina to San Francisco, where they remain homeless and destitute as Abigail fights to keep her parents, her twin brother, and herself united against all odds.
ISBN 978-0-06-227541-7 (hardback)
[1. Homeless persons—Fiction. 2. Family problems—Fiction.
3. Brothers and sisters—Fiction. 4. Twins—Fiction. 5. Faith—Fiction.
6. Swindlers and swindling—Fiction. 7. San Francisco (Calif.)—Fiction.]
I. Title.
PZ7.1.B63No 2015 [Fic]—dc23 2014037503
15 16 17 18 19 CG/RRDH 10 9 8 7 6 5 4 3 2 1
First Edition

GREENWILLOW BOOKS

To Michelle, Nora, and Ben. Of course.

BEFORE

MY KNEES ARE NUMB, BEGINNING TO BRUISE. NEXT TO ME, Aaron holds my hand—he's barely even here anymore. Mom clings to both of us like we're still little kids and in a crowd. The only things I hear are Dad's prayers, whispered to the ceiling like a secret.

I try to focus on how it will happen.

Will the room tilt?

Will everything fast-forward in a flash of light, sending us up, up, up?

Ten minutes. Five. Right now. It could happen anytime, in the blink of an eye. The trumpets will sound and then we'll all be done with the troubles of this world. Troubles we crossed the entire country to leave behind.

We're waiting. Almost thirty people kneeling on the tile floor of what used to be a convenience store. Every one of us has come from far away, swayed in some way by Brother John's promises.

I'm supposed to be happy because we are bound for a better place. For the promised land. Our true home.

I squeeze Mom's hand and then Aaron's. If I could, I'd reach for Dad, too. I squeeze until I think I'm going to break their bones, adding my own prayer—the only one I know anymore—to the hum of the room.

I'm not scared. I'm not scared. I'm not scared.

I hold on, I pray, and I wait.

ONE

WE WASH OURSELVES IN THE SINK OF A PUBLIC BATHROOM at the foot of the Golden Gate Bridge. Beside me, Mom brushes her hair without a word. I button my shirt. We don't talk about last night, or anything really. When we parked at the base of the bridge just before dawn, I watched it, lit in warm yellows and reds, and listened to the soft whisper of waves rolling into the bay.

This morning was cold and none of us talked. Not as we got dressed, or shuffled to the bathrooms. Not even now as Mom and I stand in front of the mirror, scrubbing our faces and trying to make it look as if we aren't living in our van.

"Did you sleep okay?" Mom asks.

I can barely stand to see her this way. Deflated, leftover.

"Yes," I say, but the truth is I spent the night waiting for Dad to start the van and take us home. To save us in the way God was supposed to.

Mom stares at my reflection as she tucks the brush into her purse. When she pulls her hand back out, it's holding a five-dollar bill. "I want you and Aaron to do something. Have some fun."

She offers me the wrinkled bill, our last for all I know. Before I can object, she puts it on the sink and looks away from me.

"Just take it."

I follow Aaron, trying to keep up with his long legs. Before, he'd be the one sucking air, but I haven't run in weeks. And these hills. The entire city seems designed only to go up. For a moment, I can't help but think about home. Track practice will start in a few months.

We could be back by then.

I skip every few steps to keep up with Aaron, trying to push any thoughts of North Carolina out of my head.

Dad wanted us to go with them, back to the church for prayer and maybe an answer. I was holding the five-dollar bill in my hand when he said it and I felt guilty for choosing an hour in the city over him. Mom pulled him aside and winked at us and now we're out walking by ourselves for the first time since we got here three weeks ago, the city alive and refusing to stop on all sides. North Carolina always seemed to be asleep. Here people yell and push by me and Aaron—we still aren't connected to whatever invisible current moves everyone around us.

We walk past a restaurant, its doors open, and the smell of food spilling out onto the sidewalk like an invitation. The windows are decorated with bright Christmas lights, chasing themselves around the rectangle of glass in an endless loop. If Aaron's stomach comes to life, if he's thinking about Christmas and how it passed with hardly a mention, I can't tell. He ignores the sounds of people eating brunch, the guy offering us a flyer—two T-shirts for twenty dollars—and keeps moving down the block as quickly as he can.

"Where are we going?" I ask.

He stops but doesn't turn around. He never looks at anyone anymore.

"You can go back to the van if you want."

"I don't want to go back to the van," I say. "I want to talk to you."

"Well, talk."

I almost ask him where he's going at night. If only to make him turn around, surprised to learn that I know how he slips away from the van once Mom and Dad are asleep. But he refuses to look at me, as if I'm some stray dog following him down the street.

"Did you see Dad last night?"

"I don't want to talk about Dad. Or that. Okay?"

It's the way he says *Dad*, like he's spitting something out of his mouth.

"They didn't know this was going to happen," I say.

The laugh is sharp and mean. "You think?"

"They made a mistake, Aaron."

At this, he turns around, but his eyes almost immediately drift past me, above my shoulder. Like he's seeing something coming down from the sky. His face hardens and he says, "Jesus Christ."

High above us, emerging from the fog of the city, is one of Brother John's billboards, a shocking black banner.

THE DAY OF CHRIST'S BIRTH WILL BRING JUDGEMENT

TO THIS LAND OF SIN.

THE WAY HAS BEEN PREPARED.

ARE YOU RIGHT WITH THE LORD?

CRY MIGHTILY UNTO GOD —JONAH 3:8

Brother John's website, along with the local radio station for his broadcasts, are just below the Bible verse.

I cried the whole way to California, looking away whenever we saw another one of the billboards lining the highway, encouraging us every mile we drove. Every time Dad would look in the rearview mirror, I'd hide my face. I didn't want him to see my doubt or my fear. And when we got here—when I saw Brother John for the first time, shaking Dad's hand and smiling—I forced myself to believe everything he said. But now the date has passed, and all those guarantees feel like cheap plastic silverware in my mouth.

This time I don't cry, though. I turn back to Aaron. "It doesn't matter."

I start walking away from the sign. He doesn't move.

"Doesn't matter?" Aaron says, his voice quiet. I can't tell if he's angry, sad, or maybe disappointed. He points at the black billboard and says, "That guy took everything from us and you think that doesn't matter?"

Things were already falling apart before Brother John. Dad lost his job and pretty soon he and Mom were borrowing money from Aaron and me. The first time Dad asked, I made a big fuss about it. I reminded him of all the babysitting I had done. It was close to five hundred dollars, and I wanted a car. That was before we got rid of cable and Internet. Before the yellow late-payment warnings began showing up at our front door and we started getting bags of groceries from our church. The whole time, Aaron never said a word. But when we got in the van, when we watched everything disappear out our back window, something inside of him broke.

"I'm just saying, don't let a stupid billboard ruin our day." Aaron looks at me, and then up at the sign one more time. "Let's go do something. Okay?"

We're wedged into a small table in the corner of the shop, spooning cookies and cream out of paper cups. There's barely enough room for the line of people, let alone us. But for the moment I feel normal, just a girl eating ice cream.

"This is good," I say, licking a piece of cookie off the plastic spoon. When was the last time we had ice cream? The church's end-of-summer picnic, maybe. Dad was in the dunking booth, daring Aaron to knock him into the tank of cold water while I finished my second cone.

"Like, really good."

Aaron nods, checking his iPod, plugged into the only

wall socket. He eats slowly, like he always has, and stares out the window as if he were sitting here alone. It's so obvious he's upset and I hate the silence between us, enough that I provoke him.

"I'm not stupid, Aaron."

He looks up at me and says, "I know you aren't."

"Then tell me what's going on."

He stabs at his ice cream and laughs. "Whatever could you mean?"

"Stop it. Don't be like that," I say.

"Maybe this is what I'm like now," he says.

"Oh, right. You just changed overnight. That makes total sense."

He laughs again, that same short burst. "Nothing changed last night. Including me. But if you want to talk, fine. Let's talk about how Mom and Dad have gone way off the deep end."

He stares at me, a taunt. No different than the ones he'd dangle in front of me when we were kids. Back then I'd go running to Mom, crying and yelling. As we got older, I learned to leave the room. Ignore it and him until he stopped acting like an idiot. Because I know exactly where this leads. But it's not like I have a room to leave anymore.

"Just enjoy the ice cream," I say.

He slams his cup onto the table and waves his arms around at the room, his voice rising enough to make the other people in the shop stare at us. "Are you serious? We're not on vacation here, Abs. We're living in our van. So you take a good look around and grow the hell up."

Before I can say anything—and I don't know what I'm going to say, but something—he goes on, "We need to start taking care of ourselves because—news flash!—Mom and Dad aren't up for the job anymore. We might as well be alone."

But we're not alone. We've never been alone, and that's the point. Mom and Dad have always been constant, and I want to shove that right in his face. Have it kick his memories to life like a smelling salt. Because we never had a lot, but we always had each other. They always tried. Always. And that has to still count for something.

He can see all of this on my face—I know he can—but it doesn't bring an apology. Instead he says, "And giving us five dollars of gas money so we can go eat ice cream doesn't change a damn thing. Not even close."

I have no idea where I'm going when I stand up. But I'm out the door before Aaron can scramble around the table.

He calls for me, yelling my name louder and louder as I begin to run.

Mom and Dad aren't perfect. I know this. They've made mistakes before, even if they weren't as big as moving across the country. Even if they didn't involve selling our house and everything we couldn't fit into the van.

I get it.

There have been days when the reality of what's happened to us hits me like a truck. I don't want to go to church every night. I didn't want the world to end. But no matter what happens—what will happen—Mom and Dad have never been in question for me. And he should know that.

I dodge people, trying not to worry about Aaron or why he's stopped yelling my name. For a second I think I've lost him. But on my next turn, I glance back and he's still shuffling forward, a block behind me. When I near the park, the people sprawled across the grass slapping hands and laughing, I slow down. By the time I reach the stone fence that marks the entrance, Aaron is next to me, doubled over and breathing hard.

"Jesus, what was that about?"

I still don't want to look at him or talk to him. But now

that I've stopped, Aaron jumps in front of me and forces eye contact.

"Get out of my way," I say, trying to walk around him.

He steps in front of me again. "What are you doing?"

We've always fought, even before we were born. Mom said there were times when she couldn't move because of the way we'd be carrying on inside her. But we've also always come back together. It might take an hour, or even an entire day, but somebody would crack. And then it was as if nothing had happened between us.

That's how it works. We laugh it off. But I can't.

I look away, at some kids our age sitting against the stone wall. Beside them, a man holding a trumpet is yelling, stopping every few seconds to play a few notes on his horn.

"No chilling winds! No poisonous breath!" *Berrnnnn!*

Aaron ignores him, as does everyone else.

Trumpet Man plays another loud note and yells, "I am bound!"

A few teenagers appear at the bottom of the hill, laughing. When Aaron looks at them, I make to slip past him. He sees me a second too late and tries to grab my arm, accidentally knocking me to the sidewalk.

It loosens something.

"You don't think I'm upset?" I'm crying, and I don't want to be. I've spent the last month keeping everything inside, smiling, trying to pray—pretending everything is normal. But him thinking he's the only one who is angry, who misses what we used to have, brings up words I'd normally swallow.

"You don't think I want to go home?"

"I want—"

"It's always what you want! You act like you're the only one who's allowed to be mad. Don't you think I'm mad? Do you think I like being here?"

He drops his head and won't look at me. Of course. Because that's his answer for everything now. He unplugs.

I get up, touching the growing spot of blood on my knee.

"And now my jeans are ripped. My only pair. Great."

When Aaron tries to help me, I push away his hand. I really want to push him to the ground, to make him feel something I can understand. Anything close to what's inside me. Fear and anger. Guilt. The inescapable feeling that I can't control a single moment of what's happening to all of us.

"Abs . . ." His voice is soft and apologetic, but I'm going back to the van so I can close my eyes and forget everything from last night, today—all of it. Even if only for the next hour.

"Leave me alone," I say.

I walk past him, not turning around to see if he's following.

Mom and Dad aren't in the van, and I climb all the way to the back. When Aaron enters a few minutes later, he looks surprised to see me sprawled across the backseat—his seat. But he doesn't say anything. He settles into my captain's chair and puts in his earbuds.

I turn over and face the back, my nose almost touching the worn stitching that zigzags up and down the cushion. I trace it with my finger, trying to hold on to the last gasps of anger. But it fades, leaving only regret and the hopelessness that comes with not being able to go back in time. Even if that were possible, when would I stop? Fifteen minutes? Five years? At what point in the past could I actually change what happened?

The day we sold everything—the house, all of it—people showed up early, lining up on the sidewalk and knocking on the door like they might miss their shot at the best stuff. Neither me nor Aaron could be in the house. We walked around our neighborhood all morning, barely saying a word.

When we got back, everything was gone.

I wished I believed the house and our stuff didn't matter. That was what Brother John promised every night on the radio—a new beginning. The End Times. It was what Dad said at dinner, to every person he saw at the grocery store. But when we walked back into that empty house, an undeniable piece of me was missing. Of course, Uncle Jake came and took most of the pictures, the important stuff Grandma and Grandpa gave Dad. Jake tried to stop him, too. They talked on the porch until the sun died behind them, Dad standing with his arms crossed as Uncle Jake got mad and started yelling.

That's the day I'd go back to if I could. I'd go outside and tell Dad we shouldn't go. I'd cry and scream—anything it took for him to see how big a mistake we were making. If I'd been brave enough to do that, maybe it would've worked.

Aaron clears his throat and I'm immediately brought back to the cold van. To him, sitting only a few feet from me. We no longer have the privilege of slamming a door, of being angry with any sort of distance. Of holding a grudge.

I say his name and he whips around like he's been waiting for me to make the first move. I can see the relief on his face, the regret. I could make him apologize to me right now and he would. Make him swear he'll stop being so difficult. But I don't want an apology. I want him to be normal: sarcastic, talkative. The way he's always been.

The door opens and Dad climbs inside the van. As soon as Aaron sees him, all the emotion falls from his face.

"Hey there, Gabby-Abby," Dad says. I move past Aaron and climb into Dad's arms, burying my head into his chest. I smell his aftershave, the cheap drugstore kind we were always able to afford, always with weird names like Tusk or Gentleman's Choice. Another reminder of who we were in North Carolina.

"All right now," Dad says, squeezing me tightly. "Careful. I've got those old bones."

He's always been full of words and sayings that never make sense to anyone other than him and—whenever he was around—Uncle Jake. Dad always said they were thick as thieves, and then they'd both laugh.

Dad still has his arms around me when Mom climbs in, too. She notices the tear in my jeans immediately.

"What happened? Is that blood?"

They both bend down to study the ripped material, the red scab settling across my knee. All I can think about is: this shouldn't matter. We should be able to throw these away, or at the very least buy a patch. But we can't. We have to worry about the only pair of jeans I own getting ruined.

"She fell down," Aaron says quickly. "While we were out."

He glances at me and I hope he doesn't think I'd betray him so easily.

"Yeah, I was running and I tripped," I say. "It was stupid."

Mom eyes the jeans and Dad smiles.

"It's okay, Kat," he says. "It's just a pair of jeans. The world hasn't stopped spinning."

For a moment after he says it, nobody speaks or moves. Then Aaron stands up and goes to the back of the van. The only sound is his music, tinny and barely audible from his earbuds.

TWO

BROTHER JOHN NEVER SAID WE'D BE LIVING IN OUR CAR. or that we'd hop from church to church looking for our next meal. That we'd be stuck in this city. He never said Aaron wouldn't be able to sleep or that I'd come to dream of a shower. We came all this way and there are so many things that Brother John never said would happen.

Is this what having faith means?

I study Dad's face as he leans over for Mom's hand, and she reaches back for mine. Is he still sure that this is all a part of the plan? That we are going to be okay? He smiles at me and then looks to Aaron, who is still wearing his earbuds. Dad has to tell him to come up to the other captain's chair and take my hand, to join the circle we've made. Even when we were kids, Aaron would roll his eyes and sigh loudly. He hated the long-winded church services. How the prayers always followed us home—before dinner, after our showers.

Once we're all holding hands, Dad starts to pray. His deep voice resonates through the van. He asks for strength. For the ability to love others. Then he says, "Help us, Lord. Help us know what to do next."

Aaron drops my hand.

He hasn't bowed his head or closed his eyes. He isn't even pretending today. Our eyes meet, just for a second, and I try to make him see that I don't like this either. That I am scared and tired. I want him to know that when we walked out of that church last night, I was happy to feel the cold pavement on the ground below me. To look up and see the stars, still bright against the sky.

I finally close my eyes.

I want to tell God I'm sorry for being relieved, to believe that he can help Aaron, all of us. Instead, all I can say is *please*. Over and over again. The only prayer I can manage.

✦ ✦ ✦

Despite the ice cream, my stomach aches with hunger, which makes letting the people pass in front of us that much harder. Still, I try to smile. I try to remember what Dad says—that they need it more than we do. And many of them look it. Sad and broken and bundled. I hope we don't look the same way, but after a month of lining up outside of churches for every meal, we're no different than the people we let pass in front of us. Dad just hasn't realized it yet.

"Looks like lasagna," Dad says, rubbing his hands together. He looks so happy, so grateful for whatever is underneath the steaming serving dishes. I try to imagine him the way he used to be, when school would break for the summer and he'd have us all to himself. How he always seemed to be on the verge of tears, but like it was a good thing. This is different somehow, a desperate joy. Cheap. Something you'd buy at a flea market.

"Damn. I was hoping for spaghetti," Aaron says. "Again."

Mom's voice is strained and unnatural as she reminds him that God provides everything we need. That we should be happy with what we have. To watch his language. But nothing changes on his face and whatever momentary blast of energy was fueling Mom fades, leaving her seeming just as crumpled as she's been the last twenty-four hours.

Dad doesn't falter. He puts his arm around Aaron and whispers in his ear. I watch his lips move, see Aaron become a statue, as he says, louder, "Okay, buddy?"

Aaron gives him a stiff nod and I turn away, so I don't see Aaron roll his eyes. Dismissing Dad so obviously and then both of them pretending it didn't happen.

I don't want to cry in front of all these people, so I look at the food. At the women who seem to serve us every meal, regardless of which church fellowship hall we're in. All of them white haired and smiling.

Dad straightens up and says, for all of us to hear, "Is that garlic bread I smell?"

It isn't. And all that's left of the lasagna are the overcooked pieces on the edge of the pan. The stuff nobody really wants. But as the older woman hands me a plate and a set of silverware, I try to be thankful, even for this.

We eat at a table by ourselves, the only family. Single men and the occasional woman fill the others, all of them worn and smudged with dirt, eating with their faces close to their plates. Dad finishes first, inhaling the small piece of meatless lasagna like he hasn't eaten in a week. Which might as well be true. Besides the pre-Christmas dinner one other church gave us last week—turkey, mashed potatoes with gravy—it's been sandwiches and spaghetti and whatever is easiest to mass-produce. But Dad sits here the way he would when Grandma was still alive, acting like he couldn't eat another bite if the world depended on it.

"That was good," he says. "Really good."

None of us answer, not even Mom. We stare at our plates as the room slowly begins to empty, everybody shuffling out of the small hall with a piece of fruit and a granola bar. Soon it will just be us. Dad will stand up and offer to help put the tables away. To show how grateful we are. The volunteers will laugh at his stories, the ones about him and Uncle Jake as kids. The stuff of home. The stuff I miss every single day.

When I was younger, Dad and Uncle Jake could make me believe anything. How they found a UFO in the backyard; how they caught a fish so big it dragged them underneath the lake. I held on to those stories longer than most kids would have, all of them better than any television show. And yet now, as Dad starts, all I want is for him to stop. For us to go back to the van and go to sleep. Because that's normal now.

I hand Aaron a dish. Even standing beside me he's rigid, a stranger. At home, he'd be leaning into me, trying to spray me with water. Snapping the towel at my legs, blowing bubbles into my face—whatever annoyed me most. That was his mission. Now he just stands and dries each dish like we're both making minimum wage.

"I'm worried," I say, so quiet that I barely recognize my voice. It's been hours since I last spoke. "About you."

He finishes drying the dish and stacks it on top of the rest.

"I'm fine," he says, taking the next plate from me and using his sleeve to brush the hair out of his face. When I don't pick up another plate to wash, he blows a long stream of air from his mouth.

"Be worried about them," he says, nodding at Mom and Dad before going back to the dishes. Mom works quietly and alone, folding tablecloths as if she's worried there won't be enough to do. Dad's slapping backs and picking up chairs.

"I am," I say, but Aaron doesn't say anything else, just

grabs a dish and takes my job away from me. I watch him sink a plate in soapy water before saying, "Where are you going? At night."

He pulls the plate from the water and rinses it without a word. When he starts to dry it, too, I begin to think he won't answer. That I've somehow crossed a line that never existed between us before.

"Nowhere."

I turn away from him and pick up a plate to wash. He is as stubborn as the day is long—that's what Dad would say. When we were kids, I'd get so mad at him. It burned hot inside me whenever he acted this way. But not now. This anger doesn't burn; it aches. And I don't know what to do, or how to stop him, so I finish the plate and hand it to him without a word.

"I'm fine, Abs. I promise."

"I would understand. You know I would."

Even as the words come from my mouth, I'm not sure I believe them. I don't understand, not a single bit. But I would try.

Before Aaron can answer, Dad walks into the kitchen and takes a long moment to watch us. When Aaron sees him, he starts scraping a burned piece of lasagna off one of the pans. Lately, when I'm awake before dawn and waiting for Aaron to come back from wherever he goes, I worry I'll forget who Dad was before any of us ever heard of Brother John, ever saw one of his billboards.

But it's not just me. We all need to remember what it used to be like before we came to California.

"We've been invited to church here," Dad says.

These seem to be the only words he knows anymore, and I look at the plates again, wondering what he'd do if I threw one across this kitchen—if I made a scene and refused to stop.

"So we're not going to that other place?" Aaron never says Brother John's name. He never looks Dad in the eye. Dad hesitates.

"Of course we're still going to Brother John's," he says. "You know that."

Aaron reaches across me and grabs the last plate, still covered in sauce, and dips it into the water. I wring out my washcloth, waiting for Dad to say something. To put his arm around Aaron's shoulders and make it right—even if it means not going to church tonight. Or maybe Aaron will do something. Stop washing the dishes and actually tell Dad how angry he is. Throw a fit, curse—something.

But neither of them says a thing. Aaron dries the last plate, and Dad turns to leave.

"Upstairs in fifteen minutes," he says. "Okay, guys?"

And then he's gone.

The service reminds me of home.

Nobody yells or gets out of their seat like they do when Brother John stands up to preach. Twin Christmas trees flank the altar at the front of the church, the glow of their lights making the otherwise dark room seem soft. And they sing Christmas carols I know—"O Holy Night," "Joy to the World"—simultaneously making me warm inside and ache to see our house again.

I stare at the wooden cross, suspended high against the wall at the front of the sanctuary. At home, in this exact situation, I'd probably smile. I'd close my eyes and pray to God, saying *thank you*. Every single note of the organ would wash over me until I was lifted up in the assurance I've known my entire life. Now it's like I've been disconnected. I don't know what to say to God, to anyone. And as the final hymn ends and the pastor stands up in front of us all, I bow my head more out of habit than anything else.

"Friends, we have visitors here tonight who are facing

hard times," the pastor says. He's a younger man with thinning hair and a dark beard. He smiles as he talks. "I'd like us to show them God's love in a tangible way. Give what you can, because even the smallest amount can help."

The pastor looks at us as he says this and Dad nods.

As soon as Aaron catches on, he stands up and walks down the middle aisle of the church, right through the large wooden doors that lead outside. They close loudly behind him. Mom touches me on the shoulder, as if I can somehow bring him back. As if I haven't been trying.

After a few seconds she says, "Go make sure he's okay."

She squeezes my arm and moves her feet so I can escape the tight pew. As I walk up the aisle, I dodge the men and women passing the gold collection plates back and forth in the sanctuary. People drop change, dollar bills, into the plates and smile as I pass them. They know it's for us. For me. I hurry up the aisle and out the door.

Aaron is leaning against one of the stone columns, staring into the sky. At first he doesn't say anything. But then, without turning to me, he says, "Good thing we got that in. I hate to think what might happen if we missed a chance to hear about good old Hey-Zeus."

Why can't he just believe? Now more than ever. Or at

least pretend. Even if it's just for me. Because maybe if we both pretend for a few minutes, God will see we're trying and do something. Maybe it will reconnect whatever's been cut inside of me and I'll go back to the way it used to be. Feeling God everywhere, in everything. I step closer and put my arms around him. It's so cold.

We stand there together, not talking, as people begin to filter out of the service. Some look at us, and others hurry past. Like we might hit them up for more money now that we're outside. When Mom comes up behind us, she can barely fit her arms around both of our bodies. But she still tries.

"I love you guys," she says.

"Where's Dad?" I ask.

"He's thanking the pastor," she says. "You two go get in the van. It's freezing out here."

Aaron walks away from us immediately. Behind Mom, Dad's nodding as the pastor touches his shoulder. They both bow their heads. Mom turns my face to hers.

"Go get warm. Okay?"

I wrap myself in my quilt and try to stop shivering. Aaron flips the interior light switch on and off, cursing loudly when it won't work.

"Nothing in this van works," he says, kicking the seat.

"Aaron . . ."

"What? What could you possibly say to me right now?"

He's right. I don't have anything to say. At least nothing that will fix the light or make him happy. I wrap myself deeper in the quilt and watch leaves blow across the parking lot. Aaron gives up and sits down in the backseat, pulling his sleeping bag high above his shoulders.

"What do you think they'll do with the money?" I ask.

Talking about the money embarrasses me, even though I know we need it.

"What do you think?"

"They're not going to give it to him," I say. "They can't."

Aaron laughs and then says, "Okay."

I don't know how Dad heard about Brother John, or why he sent that first check. But after he lost his job at the plant, I guess we were all looking for a sign—even if it came in the form of a billboard on the highway. Those first few months of listening to Brother John on the radio—of seeing his billboards pop up in our town—were confusing. We'd always gone to church, but this was different. I could see the excitement building inside Dad. The unpaid bills didn't matter. Mom frantically pleading with the man from the city who'd come to turn off our water wasn't a big deal. Our entire life took a backseat to this one thing.

So when they told us they'd sold the house and given the money to Brother John, that we were coming to San Francisco to have front row seats for the end of the world, I wasn't surprised. I tried to understand.

Dad said it would be an adventure—following a crooked line across the map, seeing things we'd only seen in textbooks or on television. The Mississippi River, wide and violent. The sheer length of the middle of the country. And of course we stopped at every bigger-than-life ball of twine and wax museum the road had to offer. Like the other oddities were calling to us.

And then: mountains. Breaking the skyline like teeth. Soon, these gave way to the sort of sky that only felt possible in dreams. Wide and open, just waiting to carry us away. It made the world seem small, even when we stopped at the Grand Canyon and gazed from its lip. As we stood there Dad said, "Soon this will all be gone. Amazing."

When we finally pulled into California, Dad was the only one who cheered. He made us take a family picture next to the sign on the highway, welcoming us from so far away. And when we drove into San Francisco for the first time, my chest felt like a fist.

Sometimes I think about what Dad used to tell us as kids, how having faith was like being in the ocean for too long. Sometimes you got out of the water and you were a half-mile down the beach from where you started. Only, we ended up in California. And after last night, I have no idea why we're still here.

"Are you going out tonight?" I ask. Aaron doesn't sit up. He doesn't say anything at first. "I don't know. Maybe . . probably. Don't worry about it, okay?"

I wait for him to say something else, but the only sound is the wind cutting through the van as if we aren't really here. Cars pass on the street behind us, and I look up at the broken interior light. The thing really never did work when you needed it.

This van is a map of our childhood. Fights that always seemed like the end of everything between us. Trips to the grocery store. To Niagara Falls. How we'd laugh when Dad would call it a conversion van and Aaron would playfully mock him, saying something like, "It has mini blinds! You know that's high-class!"

Aaron turns over, nearly falling off the narrow

backseat. He can't be comfortable, not with the cold air stealing through the cracks of the broken back door, held together only by a bungee cord. I spent one shivering night back there before he claimed the captain chairs were too small, that he needed to stretch his legs. When we were kids, the backseat was always prime real estate, but now even his thick sleeping bag doesn't make it warm.

"Why don't you come sit up here?"

I can barely make out his face—the brown hair, the blue eyes. My dad in all his high school pictures. Aaron twists around in the seat, facing me.

"I'm fine. Don't worry about it."

When Dad opens the door, Aaron turns back and pulls his sleeping bag over his shoulders. The rush of cold air makes me shiver again, but once Dad cranks the engine and the heat works its way through the van, my entire body relaxes. And even if it's only temporary, I don't care. It snakes around us, bringing comfort and relief. A moment of peace.

Dad adjusts his mirrors before turning his attention to a spot on the windshield. Mom comes and wraps a second quilt around me before settling into her own seat. As the van warms up, nobody says anything. The low hum of the radio and the slow hiss of the heat passing through the vents are the only sounds.

Mom clears her throat and turns around to face us. "Your father and I have decided that we won't be going to Brother John's tonight."

I sit up and stare at her. She's not like Dad, who spent our entire childhood trying to get us to believe any number of crazy things. You could always trust her to say what she meant, even when it might upset someone. She smiles and then turns to Dad, who looks skeptical.

"It's a good night to get some rest," Mom says. "Right, Dale?"

Dad hesitates, but eventually nods.

Streetlights fill the van in intermittent bursts as we loop around the block looking for a place to spend the night. A place where it's free and there won't be some train rattling past us every five minutes. Dad barely gets between two sports cars just before another car can poach the spot. And now we sit, fully aware of our lack of privacy—the inability for any of us to have a nighttime routine.

Mom pulls out the water bottle she keeps refilling. The label is gone and the plastic creaks every time she brings it out of her bag. We all get a paper cup.

"Don't get toothpaste on the seats," she says. And for some reason I can't look at her. I can't meet her eyes as she hands me my toothbrush, because of all the things to worry about.

We brush our teeth as twenty-somethings walk past our car, laughing and ready to fall into the street because of it; as two cars nearly collide, both of them riding their horns until they disappear around a corner. We brush our teeth, just like we have for years and years. For something so basic, something that should be forgettable and rote, it's everything I can do not to break down.

I hand Mom the cup and my toothbrush and I force myself to smile.

Dad is asleep, wrapped in a blanket as Mom reads by the streetlight, the front cover of her book folded around the back. When I say her name, she doesn't hesitate. She closes the book and turns to face me.

"Are you okay, sweetie? Do you need another blanket?" Before I can answer, she's taking the one off her lap and tucking it around my chair. Once she's asleep, I'll put it back on her. But for now, I let her fuss. I let her fuss over me.

"Better?"

I nod, and before she goes back to her seat, I take her arm and don't let go. We're supposed to have faith and I'm supposed to know that all of this is temporary, but the tears still pour out of me and I can't stop.

"Hey," she says, stroking my head. "Hey now. We're going to be fine. Do you hear me? Everything is going to be okay."

I fall asleep with the sound of her voice saying my name over and over again.

The backyard looks bright and warm, colored by the summer. Aaron has his baseball bat—the one he pretended was a light saber. We aren't supposed to play those types of games, the kinds where we fight and yell.

We're running together, taking cover behind a tree, the big one in the corner of our yard. I'm laughing and Aaron's frustrated; I never play the games the way he expects. Never the princess, never the one needing to be rescued by some boy with an electric sword. And then we're running again, him screaming and me smiling, toward the picnic table.

Aaron climbs on top of the table, like George

Washington in all those pictures where he's crossing the Delaware, lifting the Wiffle Ball bat high like a flag, ready to sail. To where, I can't remember. It doesn't matter. It's always someplace good.

The knock—metal on glass—comes from far away, like a bad sound effect in my dreams. And then I'm awake, squinting as lights reflect off every surface in the van. Red. White. Blue. Harsh and invasive, they highlight everything. The fake wood paneling. The small television mounted near the ceiling. Empty brown bags filled by old churchwomen litter the floor. And then us, bundled up without any excuse for why we're sleeping in a van on the side of the road. At least not a good one.

Dad rolls down his window. Somewhere in the murkiness, I remember Aaron standing on the picnic table. But then I jolt violently under the blanket, because I fell asleep before he did. I don't want to look back. I don't want to see an empty place where he should be.

The police officer is explaining about this neighborhood and how we'll need to move. Even if it was legal, he says, being this close to the park isn't safe. Dad agrees. He always agrees.

He explains our situation and it sounds so pathetic, like it's happening to somebody else.

"There are shelters," the officer says.

Behind me, Aaron stirs. Maybe he was asleep. Or maybe he slipped back into the van just now, too tricky for even the police and their harsh lights, which I wish they'd turn off already. But I still don't turn around. I can't see his face. Not now. Not as Dad starts the van and actually thanks the officer. I don't need to see his disappointment, his anger. Or worse: the validation. I don't want to see anything, so I close my eyes and try to slip back into my dream as we pull away from the curb.

BEFORE

DAD BORROWED UNCLE JAKE'S JEEP BECAUSE HE SAID HE liked to feel the mountain air. This was seventh grade, when Dad would show up with a note and a plan to get back down the mountain before Mom was off work. We drove with the top down, trying to catch the leaves that fell from the trees like tiny oblong angels. The wind muted everything; I couldn't hear anything Dad or Aaron said; I could only watch them smile and laugh as we climbed the mountain.

I was lost—happily, completely—so I never saw the clouds.

Aaron looked at his arm, and then to the sky. By the time I felt the first drop, it was pouring. Just like that—one drop, and then a thousand. All three of us were screaming as Dad pulled the Jeep into a rest area, deserted and overgrown—nothing more than a few picnic tables and one ancient vending machine. I jumped off the back of the Jeep as soon as he parked and ran for the tables, sheltered by a couple of huge pine trees. It was still dry underneath them and I stood there, shivering and watching as Dad pulled a blanket from under the seat and came running with Aaron across the small parking lot.

"Put this around you," he said, handing me the quilt. He had another one for Aaron and we stood there, eventually getting warm underneath those huge trees.

In front of us, the rain fell like a sheet. Dad wiped his forehead as he watched, finally saying, "We probably should have taken the van."

Aaron laughed first, but Dad and I didn't need much encouragement. We stood there laughing like fools, watching the rain fall harder than I'd ever seen before.

"Are we going to go back to school?" Aaron asked. Dad shook his head.

"We aren't going anywhere until it stops raining," he said. "And the Jeep dries enough that we don't get our rear ends soaked."

Ten minutes went by with nothing but rain and, in the distance, a small rumble of thunder. Dad looked to the sky, as if he couldn't believe it was happening, and finally said, "You guys hungry?"

I didn't want to get back in the Jeep, even if there was a restaurant close. The idea of sitting in a booth, soaked to the bone, made me wrap the quilt tighter around my shoulders.

"I'll set some traps," Aaron deadpanned. "Abs, you build a fire."

He feigned a break for the woods, and I smiled.

"I was thinking more vending machine and less hunter-gatherer," Dad said, smiling.

He grabbed Aaron in a headlock, laughing as he struggled to get away. And when Aaron did escape, when he tried to wrestle Dad to the wet ground, they both laughed even harder.

We spent the next hour eating Cheez Doodles and tortilla chips, washed down with a painfully weak fruit punch. With the last quarters Dad could find, we got chocolate chip cookies. The three of us, sitting on the picnic bench with a blanket over our heads—passing the bags back and forth until the rain stopped.

THREE

WHEN I WAKE UP THE NEXT MORNING, DAD IS GONE AND Mom is trying to organize the various cups and bags that have accumulated in the front seat. I watch her for a few minutes before I say, "Where's Dad?"

She pauses. "He went to talk with Brother John. He'll be back in a little while."

I sit up and try to stretch the discomfort out of my neck. I used to love sleeping in the van whenever we'd go visit Grandpa and Grandma. Waking up as we were pulling into their driveway turned time into something that could be manipulated, bent.

Mom hands me a banana and I take a small bite, watching people walk from their cars into Safeway. We parked in the lot last night. The bright lights and, as the morning came, the constant opening and closing of car doors made it difficult to stay asleep. But at least it kept Aaron with us. He's still in the backseat. Every few seconds, he breathes out in a tiny whistle.

"Mom?" She turns to me, trying to smooth a wrinkled brown paper bag. "Could we do something fun today?"

The first two weeks here were like a vacation. Or at least, a church trip. During the day we explored the city. We walked across the Golden Gate Bridge and went to Fisherman's Wharf. We still punctuated each day with a church service, Brother John's excitement growing larger every night, but at least it felt almost normal. Then the trips to see the cable cars ended and it was Brother John all day, every day. Now that God decided not to come, maybe we can get a small part of those first days back.

"Well, we can ask your father," Mom says, still busy with the bag.

"We don't have to spend any money," I say. "I just want to do something."

Mom puts the bag down and comes to kneel in front of me. She touches my cheek and stares at me for a few moments before saying, "Do you want to go into the store and get yourself something to eat? I think they have pancakes on the hot bar. We have some extra money now."

"I'm good with this," I say, holding up the banana. Not that it will be enough, because it won't. But I want every dollar of that money to take us home. To put gas in the tank and miles between us and this city. I don't need pancakes. I can live without pancakes.

"You could go out for a run before he gets back," she says. "Maybe you could get Aaron to go, too."

I give her a look and we both laugh. She puts her hand over her mouth, trying to stifle the sound. Then she says, "I can dream."

Dad always joked that Aaron got his family's good looks and Mom's lack of athletic ability. Either way, I was the only athlete in the family—even if I haven't been able to run consistently in a month.

But a run—a chance to forget for even a little while—sounds good.

When I go to put on my running shoes, Mom says, "Don't go too far. I don't want to lose you."

I circle the block five times, trying to push myself faster whenever I see the van. Mom waves each time I pass, the way she would whenever she came to one of my track meets. That always made Dad and Aaron crazy—*She can't wave to you, Kat. She's racing!*—but she still did it every time I made it around the track.

If we were at home, I'd be running five, six miles a day. Track practice officially starts in March, but the informal training sessions have already begun. We had the best four-hundred-meter relay team in the state, or that's what people were saying. When Coach Decker told me about the first training session, I shrugged and said I needed to go to class. I hated blowing her off, but what was I supposed to say? *My dad thinks the world's about to end, so I'll probably miss it. But good luck this year!*

I slow down to a walk as the sidewalks begin to fill with people on their way to work. I stand to the side, stretching my leg against the window ledge of a restaurant, watching everyone pass.

Kids, off for winter break, walk with their parents. They scream and point into store windows, too excited to contain themselves. When we first got here, I kept track of the days—the time. Every minute brought something new, something I hadn't seen before. Now the days blur together, a collection of unfocused moments that repeat one after another. Sleep, eat, Brother John.

When my legs feel loose, I walk again. People push past me, on their cell phones or talking to friends. I smell their coffee, the breakfast burritos in their hands. I listen to their conversations about hating their bosses, the Christmas presents they received. It's all so normal, and it makes me feel like more of an outsider.

I start running again, even harder.

Dad is leaning against the hood of the van, one foot resting on the bumper. He shields the sun from his eyes with his hand, as if he's saluting. As soon as he sees me, he waves.

"How was it?" he asks.

"I'm out of shape," I say, poking him in the stomach. His paunch was already gone before we left, but this empty stomach full of ribs still makes me pull back my finger quickly.

"You could come with me next time," I say.

I half expect him to say something about living forever. About God and how we won't need to worry about our bodies for much longer. Instead he laughs and says, "I think I'm more than a little out of shape, Gabs."

I think for a second before saying, "We can go slow."

He nods, not answering me. I don't expect him to come run. Not really. But at this point, I'd take it. Anything other than the constant refrain of church services which have stolen so much of who he used to be. There were times when he would stay home to watch football on Sundays, skipping church and telling Mom that God didn't mind—that the Bears needed him. That was years ago, but I'd give anything to have that guy standing in front of me right now.

"Gabs, if I tried to run right now, it wouldn't be slow as much as it would be dead."

I put my head down and laugh. I don't know why I'm embarrassed.

"Can we do something today?" I ask. "Anything. I just can't sit in the van all day again."

Dad buttons his jacket and watches a train pass through a busy intersection on the next block. I ready myself for disappointment. For him to smile and begin with *Well, Brother John. . .* I don't even need to finish the thought, because that would be it. Our entire day, sucked into the black hole of preaching and prayer.

Dad gives me a look, clever like a cat, and says, "Well, what are you thinking, Gabs?"

✦ ✦ ✦

Aaron and I walk down the cold beach, shoes off and hands stuffed deep into our pockets. Mom and Dad are far ahead of us, talking.

"It's freezing out here," I say. Aaron kicks a seashell toward the water and nods. "I thought beaches were supposed to be warm."

We walk together like that, my feet slipping under the sand. When he stops to tie his shoelace, I say, "I'm surprised you're not dead, having to stay in the van all night."

I want it to be funny. I want him to smile.

But all he says is, "I'm okay."

"Okay? That's it?"

He stands up, brushing the sand from his palms. "I don't know what you want me to say."

I think he's going to start walking down the beach again. Instead he picks up a seashell and throws it into the coming waves. He's gotten so good at erasing the emotion from his face, his body. Even now, he looks bored. As if we were sitting in World History listening to Mr. Burns drone on about Stalin.

"Don't you care?"

Aaron faces me, his face red from the wind. "Of course

I care, Abs. That's not the point. I can care all day long and it doesn't make a difference. It's you who needs to realize who Mom and Dad are now."

"So that's it? They make one mistake and it's over?"

"Jesus, why do you defend them?" Aaron says. "This isn't a mistake. They fucked up. Big-time. And you act like you can't even see it."

"Of course I see it! But what am I supposed to do? Run away every night? Because that's really going to show them. That fixes everything."

Aaron turns away from me, sticking his hands in his pockets as he walks. I grab his shoulder. "You're so full of crap, you know that?"

"Well, I'm rubber and you're glue," he says.

How many times has he cracked a joke or slipped in a sarcastic comment at the exact right moment? Things I never could or would say to Mom and Dad. But this is different. It's dismissive, which is so much worse.

It's not like I'm ignoring how bad things are. Every night, as we fall asleep in the van, I cannot escape the fact that our parents have ruined everything. That's true. But we have a choice—all of us. We can spend every day looking for reasons to snipe, to pick and pull at what little we have left until it's nothing but crumbs. Love and family, in the ruins. Or we can fight to stay together. To refuse to knock each other down with what we say—or what we don't.

I sit down in the sand and stare out at the water, violent and beautiful at the same time. Aaron sits next to me, but he doesn't say anything. Behind us, Dad yells. We both look at him.

"I think things can get back to normal," I say.

"We were never normal," Aaron says.

His eyes track Dad, coming down the beach now. He's right, of course. We've never been normal. We've always been different, and that's what I love. It's as if nobody else could crack the code of what it meant to be a part of our family, a gift given only to us. Aaron used to think that, too. But now, whenever I look at Aaron, all I see is the anger clouding over his face. I force myself to change directions. To not let our entire relationship become something different.

"Well, you're acting pretty normal," I say. "A big sourpuss."

He shakes his head. "God. Sourpuss? Really?"

I punch him and fix my face into a pitiful frown. "That's

how you look. All sad, like you want to cry."

I can see his expression changing, the way he's fighting the smile I imagine is trying to push through—pressing against every wall he's put up. I punch him a second time and he gives me this look, like I've finally turned on a switch somewhere inside him.

"Watch it," he says.

"Or what?" I smile.

"Or I'll put you in that water quicker than you can scream." He jumps to his feet. "That's what."

He's got my hand before I can stop him. We circle each other, him going for my other hand and me trying to jump backward at the same time. I look at the water, rough and cold. All I can think about is it creeping through my clothing, grabbing my skin. About how strong he is.

I tell myself he wouldn't really throw me in.

"Mom will kill you," I say, just to make sure.

"I'll take my chances."

And then he's got me on his shoulder, carrying me toward the water. All I can do is scream. I yell at Aaron. I yell for Dad. But the ocean is too loud and Aaron is unstoppable at this point.

"That old man can't help you. I'll throw him in, too!"

Dad says something again, and this time it sounds like he's laughing, too. I'm sure Mom's worried about hypothermia and pneumonia and whatever else might be hidden in the water. But Dad will calm her down.

That doesn't mean I want to go under.

I hang from Aaron's shoulder as he wades into the ocean. I try to lift my legs higher, but the water still jumps up and catches my foot, making me yelp. Aaron laughs, going deeper—enjoying every minute.

"You know I love you, Abs," he says.

And he drops me.

The water envelops everything, cutting me off from the rest of the world. I stay submerged for a second, taking in the peace and quiet as the cold grips my body and steals my breath. Everything could be different when I stand up. Even if I don't know why or how it will happen.

Mom is too busy wrapping what's left of our dry towels around every part of my body to worry about Dad and Aaron, who are still cackling at the way I grabbed Aaron's ankle and pulled him under. How he came running out of the ocean like it was on fire.

"You kids," Mom says, going at my hair with another

towel. She glares at Dad. "And you're no better."

Dad grins, ringing out his shirt. Aaron tried to throw him into the water, too, but couldn't. It took both of us—me pretending to need help finding my footing and Aaron sabotaging him from behind.

"They're just having fun," Dad says. "Kids being kids."

"That's my point! You're just as bad!" I can't tell if she's really upset or if she's pretending, but her face is tight and she doesn't look at Dad when she says, "And now we don't have any dry towels."

Dad looks at her and then nudges Aaron. "Son, I think your mother needs a hug."

Mom's hands stop working the towel. Aaron stands, dripping wet.

"Aaron Parker, I swear—"

"You look stressed, Mom. Come here. Give me a hug." Aaron comes closer, fueled by Dad's laughter and Mom's shriek. She jumps behind me and says, "Dale!"

"Hug your son, Kat!"

"You don't want to hug me, Mom?"

She turns and runs for the van, locking the door behind her and refusing to get out until Dad has apologized a hundred times and Aaron has the last dry towel wrapped around his body. I finish drying my hair, watching her through the dirty windows of our van. When she finally unlocks the doors, she shakes her head and pushes Dad away from her, still playing at being angry. But when Dad opens his arms, she goes to him and puts her head on his chest.

If I could, I would freeze this moment and never let any of us leave. We could live on this beach, freezing and wet, but happy.

Mom holds a towel under the hand dryer, muttering to herself. The other towels sit in a wet lump on the sink's counter. Nobody else is in the bathroom, which is tagged with spray paint and looks the way you'd expect a free bathroom at the beach might. But the heater is turned up high and I couldn't ask for much more.

"Your father . . ." She says it like he forgot to take out the trash. "These towels are never going to dry."

She sighs, but keeps the towel under the hot air. I'm on the counter, studying her.

"It's nice," I say. "Being happy here."

She looks at me strangely. "What does that mean?"

"I don't know. It's just been . . ."

She stops drying the towel and puts a hand on my knee. "You choose if you're happy. Only you can let somebody take it away from you, Abigail."

"You're right," I say.

But I'm not sure she is. Someone snuck off with our happiness. Was it Brother John? That is the easy answer, and probably the correct one, too. But Aaron isn't wrong when he says that Mom and Dad made choices to put us here. They're accountable, and I hate myself for thinking it. No matter how true it is.

Outside, Dad and Aaron are leaning against the van. Dad is talking to Aaron, who seems happy. When they see us, Dad leans over and bumps Aaron with his shoulder.

"We could've helped," Dad says, pointing to the still-damp towels in Mom's hand.

"Not with these," Mom says, lifting up the wet pile of towels. "Hopeless."

"We could go to the Laundromat," Dad says. And then they share this look, one so familiar it turns my stomach. It says, *We have to be careful. There's so little left.* And I immediately feel guilty for thinking they aren't suffering, too. For taking that five-dollar bill from Mom yesterday and wasting it on ice cream.

I try to shake those feelings away, and take the towels from Mom.

"Watch," I say, reaching up and putting them across the luggage rack on the roof of the van. It was a trick I learned when our youth group went on a mission trip once. Granted, that was in Tennessee during the summer. But it could still work.

"There you go, Gabs," Dad says, coming and taking a few towels from my arms. Mom does the same. Then, finally, Aaron. We lay the towels on top of the van until it resembles a large paper-mache project. Something we would've done in elementary school. After we're finished, we stand there looking at the van. It's freezing, and I can't stop shaking. Dad puts his arm around me and squeezes.

We don't start the van, but being out of the wind makes it immediately warmer. I sit next to Aaron in the backseat, both of us under his sleeping bag like we would do when we were kids. Up front, Mom and Dad talk directions and what church is serving when. But we don't move. We sit in the van, the sound of waves breaking in the distance. I start to get lost in the sounds when Aaron, eyes still closed, says, "That was fun."

"I told you," I say, punching him in the shoulder.

"Yeah, you're a total genius," he says, easily blocking the next punch I throw. Sitting next to each other, it feels like we could beat anything. And I think: This is it. Everything I want to believe in. Because right now, I feel complete.

"Promise me you won't sneak out of the van tonight," I say softly.

Aaron flinches. He closes his eyes for a long time. When he opens them again, he looks at Mom and Dad. I'm worried I ruined whatever was mended.

I glance quickly at the sky—so Aaron won't see me—and think, *Please*.

Aaron keeps staring at Mom and Dad.

"Why do you care?" he murmurs back. "I'm not getting in trouble. I'm not in any danger."

But how would I know? He won't tell me anything, and no matter what he says, being in the city alone at night is a risk.

We don't need risks. Not now.

I don't want to start another argument, but he doesn't

understand the way it feels each time he leaves, like I'm losing a body part. And whether that's fair or not, it's real.

"One more night. For me."

We can start there and move forward. One night after the next, until it feels normal again. Aaron waits and then nods once before he finally says, "Okay."

FOUR

BROTHER JOHN STANDS AT THE FRONT OF THE ROOM, NOTHING but four whitewashed walls and a single cross on a nail. He stands defiantly, holding the Bible high above his head, but looking at the ground, as if he is thinking deeply about how to start the sermon. Behind us, a man encourages him: "Help him, Lord!"

"Do not fear," he says, finally looking up, his eyes a deep blue, like water. He's wearing the same suit he always does—cheap and black, except for the elbows, which have turned gray with age. I've never seen him in anything else.

He smiles and intones, "That's God's word, now. Do not fear."

A few hands go into the air, palms up to the ceiling

as Brother John sweeps his hand across the makeshift sanctuary, pointing the Bible at every person still here. The first night we came into this room, I was surprised thirty people could make it feel so cramped. It was as if they were stacked on top of one another, like the folding chairs we all sat on. The room felt electric, alive. Now there were maybe ten left, but Brother John still preaches with the same passion. The same urgency.

"I know you're scared. But we aren't following my plan. Thank goodness, no." Brother John slaps the Bible against his thigh and then holds it high above his head. "This is God's plan! You, me—all of us. Sitting here right now. That's God's plan."

Aaron's eyes are stuck to the wall above Brother John's shoulder. Beside him, Dad has his hands in the air, agreeing with every word Brother John says. When my eyes go to Mom, she smiles and discreetly nods my attention back to Brother John.

"But there is good news," Brother John says. "Do you want to hear it?"

They do. Everyone in the room begins to yell. They've come from so far away—and they've stayed—to hear the good news Brother John is peddling.

"God isn't done with any of us. Not even close."

Dad stands up, kicking his chair behind him. It almost hits a woman and her small child, but nobody seems to notice. It starts a chain reaction and people are jumping up from their seats, dropping to the floor—the room is falling apart person by person. Aaron scoots closer to me, just an inch.

"That's right! I never said this was going to be easy! I never said there wouldn't be a test!"

Brother John goes to Dad, gripping both sides of his face—the way a professional wrestler might—and says, "God is coming for you, Brother Dale! Do not fear!"

When he lets go, Dad collapses in a heap. Before he even hits the floor, Brother John is at the back of the room, moving quicker than I thought he could, grabbing other people by the head and watching as they fall. He swings back toward us, but Mom pulls both me and Aaron to the floor, her hands tight around my arm. She's whispering something I can't make out as we lay there. Brother John stands above us, his arms spread wide like he's trying to embrace the entire room.

"Brothers and sisters—God hasn't forgotten us. He's planning something special right now. All I need to know is: Do you believe?"

Dad's voice is the first to fill the room, like he's ready to cry. Soon everybody is yelling with him, choking on screamed responses. Mom grips my hand, her eyes also closed. But it's different than Dad, who lies on the floor with his face pressed against the cold tile—lips moving like hummingbird wings.

Brother John falls to his knees, his palms extended toward us. Slowly the room grows silent, nothing but our breath and the slow hum of a fan somewhere in the building. The sound is familiar. I'd hear it whenever I would sneak into the sanctuary of our old church in North Carolina. Dad was always volunteering and I'd go, disappearing when nobody was paying attention. I'd escape the heat during the summer, lying on the soft red cushioned pews of the balcony listening to the loud silence of the cavernous room.

Brother John's voice is low, but still a shock.

"God, I'm not going to talk anymore. You know we're waiting. You know we aren't going anywhere, Lord."

I listen for Dad's voice, hoping that he won't agree. But his voice is so loud, so determined. I'd know that "Amen" anywhere.

✦ ✦ ✦

When we get to the van, Aaron sits in Mom's seat and stares at the church like it might stand up and run away. He reaches over and turns on the van, cranking the heat high. The intensity is beautiful. We used to convince Uncle Jake to take us for rides in the back of his old Jeep, the top down even though it was winter. When he'd drop us off back at home, those first few steps inside the house felt exactly this way. But soon the heat becomes oppressive and the van starts to sputter. I move up to Dad's seat and turn off the ignition.

"What are you doing?" Aaron says, still staring at the church.

"We can't waste the gas. And besides, I was about to melt."

Aaron blows air through his lips. I pull my knees between the steering wheel and my chest. The van is already colder.

"They're never going to change," he says.

I don't say anything, because I saw the way Dad ran up to Brother John after the service. They're sitting in his office right now, talking. I was relieved when Mom handed us the keys. I've never felt comfortable around Brother John, or understood the draw. Same suit. Same words. Same everything. He doesn't look like any other pastor we've ever had before. They all dressed nicely, like businessmen. Brother John dresses like a man running out of time. Nothing's ever ironed and there are stains on his lapel, on his tie—which never lasts too long around his neck. Nothing about him makes sense.

"What do you think they're talking about in there?" I ask.

"Jesus."

"Seriously."

"What else would they be talking about?" he says. "That's all they ever talk about."

It's true, of course. Brother John never asks how we're doing. He never invites us over for a meal or offers a shower. All he's ever done is invite us to church.

The doors of the building open and light pours into the parking lot. The people who leave look different than the ones who arrived. Newer, fresher—I can't say why. And that's how I want to feel. It's something I've never been able to explain to Aaron, even when we weren't living in our van. But I ask myself: Would I take it right now? Would I swallow a pill—say a prayer—that makes me forget everything? That lets me be as happy and confident as everybody coming through those doors?

Dad and Mom appear in the doorway. Mom is wearing his jacket, covering the wool coat she's had forever. Aaron looks at them and then back to me.

"Don't forget why we're here, Abs."

Dad steps in front of the van, doing the thing where he's trying to seem mad but everybody knows it's a joke. Sometimes he even wags his finger, which always gets him laughing more than us. Mom reaches for the door and Aaron is already up and moving to the back, that now-familiar vacant disappointment haunting his face. Dad knocks on the window.

"Are you trying to freeze your old man to death?"

He smiles and I unlock the door. As he climbs in, I look to the back. Aaron is already zipped up and invisible in the shadows.

FIVE

AARON doesn't say a word as we drive around looking for a spot to spend the night. But Dad and Mom won't stop talking. Slowly, their voices begin to lower and the hum of the wheels on the road along with the radio, turned down until it's just a rumor of sound, are a drug. I try to keep my eyes open, to focus on something other than the slow pull of sleep dragging me toward unconsciousness.

I wake up startled, like a gun went off. Nobody in the van is moving, so I try to calm myself and find a comfortable place to rest my head against the cold window. I look out for a minute, and it's as if the entire city is frozen.

I turn around out of habit. When we were kids, I used

to get up in the middle of the night and walk to Aaron's room. I'd turn on the lights and check to make sure he was still close.

As we got older, I wasn't allowed to come into his room anymore. First he put up signs, warnings to stay out—that sort of thing. A few years later it was implicit. He expected the space, and I gave it to him. I used to tell him I couldn't get into his room even if I wanted to. The place was always a pit; that's what Mom would say. But sometimes I'd still wake up and hear him moving around his room. That was enough. Now all I have to do is turn my head and he's there, usually with his earbuds in, staring out the window.

His sleeping bag is spread across the backseat. Clothes are scattered across the floor, along with a few books. I know he's probably going to be mad, but I get out of my seat and, dodging the paper bags littered on the floor, walk quietly to the back of the van.

When I touch where his shoulder should be, it's too soft.

No.

He's watching right now, I tell myself—this is one of his jokes, like throwing me in the ocean. I don't want him to have broken his promise. But when I pull back the sleeping bag, all I find is a sweater and a few shirts manipulated to look like his body.

I look from the sleeping bag to the clothes to the back door. The surge of anger is so awful and alive inside me I could scream. And maybe I should. Maybe I should yell as loud as I can, waking up Mom and Dad—this whole block—because then we'd just have to deal with it. We'd wait here until Aaron got back and we'd finally have a real discussion about everything that's happening. Everything that's happened.

Loyalty is the only thing that keeps me quiet. That and the satisfaction I'll feel when he comes back into the van and finds me, awake and angry. I rework his sleeping bag into a body and swivel my captain's chair so it faces the rear of the van—I'll be the first thing he sees when he sneaks back in.

But as I sit there, it doesn't seem like enough.

When I stand up, I tell myself I'm just going to sit in the backseat—to scare him even more, maybe. But when I got to there, all I can think about is the mock body inside his sleeping bag and how much I want to show him that he isn't the only person who wants to run away.

I slowly unpeel the duct tape and silently remove the

cardboard from the window, my heart running crazy in my chest. From there it's easy to unbind the cord and open the door. As it swings open, I throw a look at Dad, half expecting him to spring from his seat. Even my breathing seems too loud. But he and Mom are both still passed out in the front seat as I lower myself onto the street.

I have no plan, and at first I think I'll just wait in one of the shadows that fill the corners of the street. But the cold cuts through my sweatshirt, so I start walking—only to the end of the block, I tell myself. Streetlights spill onto the sidewalk every few feet like yellow puddles. The street is empty, but I still move cautiously because who knows what's hiding ahead, anywhere.

As I turn the first corner, things become familiar. That one bike shop. The fast food restaurant on the corner. Ahead, I see the entrance to the park.

Even as I walk, I can't stop myself from shivering. I should go get my jacket, but I'm afraid I'll wake up Mom and Dad. Or maybe I'm afraid that if I go back inside the van, I won't have the nerve to leave again. So I start to jog, slowly at first. It doesn't take long to get warm, and soon my heart is like one of those cars that passes in the night, booming and throbbing deeply as I push forward.

I should turn left, shorten my route to just a block. But my momentum takes me up and down the nameless streets; left, right, and then left again. I let the air struggle down my throat and into my ragged lungs. I'll probably pay for running twice in one day when I wake up and my legs are stiff like boards. Right now, though, with the cold night air against my face and the tall buildings rising above me like sentries, I wonder if this is why Aaron leaves.

I let everything fall out of my mind. All I think about is my feet pounding against the sidewalk. Trying to let my breath slip in my nose and out of my mouth. To pump my arms like machines. I only stop when I turn another corner and see two people standing down the block.

They are misshapen, like something from a nightmare. One looks about ten feet tall, long and gangly. He leans back and then forward, but I can't figure out why. The other is short, like a child, but stockier. The smaller one says, "Yo, you're getting that shit on me."

The other, standing on the hood of the car, laughs and says, "It ain't shit, dude."

"Well that doesn't mean I want it on me. Keep on target. And besides—" He stops talking and, I think, looks right at me. My eyes finally focus and I see the two of them, maybe a few years older than me, a bit more clearly. The smaller one is kneeling next to a large SUV, a can of spray paint in his hands. The other is peeing into its open sunroof.

The taller one jumps from the hood and yells, "Who's that? Teller?" It doesn't sound threatening, more the way you'd greet a friend you see across the street. But I don't wait to hear what comes next.

My legs tremble with each step, but I go hard and fast even though suddenly nothing seems familiar. Every shadow reveals another person wrapped in newspaper or a stained blanket, all of them groaning and yelling at the night and me, rushing by faster than I thought possible. The voices of the two guys fade behind me, and I don't stop running—faster and faster—until I'm back on what looks like a main street. I feel like I'm going to throw up, but I keep moving until something familiar rises out of the darkness.

I know this place.

The tall stone walls and metal gates. Rows of empty cement bleachers stretch down to the empty field. Every time we passed it, Dad would say, "A football stadium right in the middle of the city . . . how do you like that?" I'm two blocks away from the van, maybe three. Regardless, close enough to sprint.

Behind me something scrapes the pavement and I don't even think, I put up my fists—even if they're useless—and swing.

I connect with something fleshy and hard. It hurts, but I'm ready to swing again until I hear Aaron's voice and see him shielding the eye I probably just blackened.

"Abs, what the hell?"

My fist is still raised and my entire body ready to react. He's sweating, too, almost panting for breath. My initial relief is taken over by anger.

But it's like he can't see anything I'm feeling, or doesn't remember what he promised. Because all he does is stare at me and say, "Christ, who are you? Muhammad Ali?"

I don't ask how he knows about the opening in the fence that surrounds the football stadium, or why he hasn't shown it to me before. I don't ask how he knew I was here, or why he was out of breath. I follow him down into the belly of the stadium, toward grass so green it seems plastic, unreal. He lies right in the middle of the field, patting the spot next to him.

"I came back to the van," he says when I lay down on the wet grass. "You weren't there and I freaked. You can't do this, Abs. You can't be out here by yourself."

Above us, the clouds drift across the moon, making everything seem darker than it really is. Aaron goes up on his elbow and stares down at me. I close my eyes.

"I know I said I wouldn't leave," he says.

I take almost a minute before I finally answer him. "That's right. You did."

What he says next isn't what I expect.

"I didn't pinky-dog swear." I open my eyes and stare at him. Pinky-dog swearing was about as serious as you could get when we were kids. It held more weight than anything else—friends, fights, parental decrees. If you pinky-dog swore, you were bound. I don't even remember who came up with it or why it held such reverence. It just did.

But now it feels like a gimmick.

"I didn't think I had to," I say.

Aaron's face falls a bit. "You didn't. I—it's complicated, Abs. Okay?" He lies back down on the grass, our arms barely touching.

Of course it's complicated. Nothing is simple. Not anymore. Everything has twisted and turned and now our problems are thicker than a blackberry bush in August. But that doesn't mean we can't start pruning away one thorny branch at a time. It doesn't mean we can just run away. I sit up and I say, "I don't understand what's happening."

He doesn't move, just lies there with his arm draped over his eyes. Like he's trying to disappear. "Do you trust me? Like, with anything?"

Of course. Always and with everything. Even when he does stuff like this, we're connected. That's always been the point. That's what I want him to see with Mom and Dad.

"You know I do."

"What if I told you I'm going to leave?"

I'm confused and I know my voice shows it when I say, "Leave?"

"If we could go right now, would you? Would you go back home?"

Habit tells me to send a prayer, something quick and silent, shooting into the sky—but I'm not sure that will help anymore. But if we could go home? If Dad woke up tomorrow morning and said, "All right. We're leaving"?

The happiest day of my life. It's so obvious, how could he even ask?

He rushes on, his words coming fast.

"We need to leave, because Mom and Dad never will," he says. "They're going to keep going to that church and spend every night in that van for the rest of their lives. Hear what I'm saying, Abs. They're never taking us home, and we need to get out of here."

I shake my head.

"I don't have it all planned yet, but you need to be ready."

I stand up, but I don't know what to do. I can't walk away, but I can't form a response either. All I can say is, "You're acting like an idiot. You know that, right?"

"Hey," he says, standing up and taking my arm. I try to pull away, but he won't let me. "I know you want to go home. Me, too. That's what I'm talking about. Going back to school. Seeing our friends. Uncle Jake. Tell me you don't want that."

"I want all of us to go home," I say.

"Me, too," he says. "But they're not going anywhere—you saw them tonight."

Aaron drops his hands to his sides and opens his mouth, as if he's already planned for whatever argument I'm going to offer next. But I don't have one because he's talking about abandoning Mom and Dad—something I have never considered to be part of the discussion. Thinking about it lights a new flame of indignation.

"How are we going to get home?"

"I haven't figured that part out yet," he says.

"Of course you haven't. Of course."

"Are you saying I'm wrong? You want to be here?"

"You won't leave," I say, dismissing him.

Aaron doesn't answer. It only makes me madder.

"Fine. Then I'm telling Mom and Dad."

The words feel childish in my mouth, something I should've outgrown. But what else can I do? How else can I respond? I wait for him to come back with something—to give me any reason why this is a good idea, our only choice. He stands there, annoyingly silent.

"If you're not going to say anything, I'm heading back."

Still, nothing. So I start to move, and he stops me. "Wait."

I do. For an entire minute as he stands there, kicking at the grass and trying to figure out how to sell me on what is easily his most ridiculous idea ever. Leaving. As if we would steal a car and drive it cross-country like some kind of terrible movie.

"Really, I don't even know what this means," I say.

"It means I can't lose you to him, too," Aaron finally says. "I won't. So we need to get out of here, because I'm terrified you're going to end up exactly like Mom and Dad."

"That won't happen," I say quietly.

"I can't take that chance—for either of us, Abs. We need to go. And if you won't come with me, I'll go alone. I really will."

His words hit me like bullets, one after another, lodging themselves in my chest. Making me bleed. If Aaron left, I'd have no idea how to move, which way to go—how to function at all.

"We can go to Mom and Dad," I repeat.

Both his voice and face go hard. "And tell them what?"

Aaron looks tired, as if he just carried me up one of these San Francisco hills. I keep opening my mouth but nothing comes out. Because what can I say? He's right about Mom and Dad. We shouldn't have to tell them this. They should know.

But is that it? Is that the final answer? They make a mistake and we leave?

"Can we go back to the van?" I say.

He nods, but not before he says, "I'm being serious, Abs. You need to be ready for this. Because I'm going with or without you."

BEFORE

THE MOON WAS HIGH IN THE SKY, THE KIND DAD ALWAYS SAID you catch if you jumped high enough. I couldn't stop giggling. Aaron was frustrated.

"Will you shut it? You're going to get us caught."

"They can't hear us from all the way in the house," I said. "Even if I stood on that stump and yelled, "Help! Help!" they wouldn't hear. They're dead to the world in there."

Aaron shook his head and said, "Hey, this is your party. But go ahead and do that if you want to see Dad come running with a baseball bat."

"Well, he doesn't have a bat, so . . ."

"Jesus, Abs. A frying pan, then. The point remains: shut up."

I smiled into the dark night as we tromped through the field behind our house. The grass was knee high, itching my legs and hiding the footpath that led to the pond. We hadn't been here for years.

When we were kids—when we never would have considered leaving the house after dark—this field was the biggest inconvenience we faced. Five minutes to walk, but less than two if you ran.

Aaron wouldn't run, though. Not anymore. So we walked, going slower than we ever would've thought possible as kids. When every second spent out of the pond was considered wasted.

"I can't believe you talked me into this," Aaron said. "The pond is nasty, in case you don't remember. Like, really disgusting."

"That's the fun," I said, leaning my shoulder into his. "It's like science!"

That made him laugh. "Yeah, something like that."

When we finally came to the pond, I stopped. Even in the moonlight, I saw the green film lying across the water, which, as Aaron pointed out, was never particularly clear in the first place. But it was as if someone had dumped a giant bowl of rotten oatmeal on top of the normal coating of green. The only visible water ran up against the small banks, as if it were trying to escape the slime.

"I bet, if we're really careful," Aaron said, "we'll only need one shot of penicillin when we're finished."

I hit him, because it wasn't funny. Of course he was laughing.

"Hey, what are you waiting for? Dive in, Abs. Looks refreshing as hell."

I knew it was stupid to be upset, because it was just a pond and we could go and swim anytime we wanted at the public pool. But when I'd gone into Aaron's room earlier that night and convinced him to come with me, it felt like a secret. The kind we used to keep when we were younger. And now it was over. He'd go back to his room and call one of his friends, spending all night on the phone.

"Hey," he said. "Are you upset?"

"Yeah. I'm really mad at the algae," I said.

Aaron looked at the pond and gave it the middle finger. "You see that, algae? That's what I think of you."

"Aaron . . ."

He turned to face me, smiling as he said, "Algae don't care. It's science."

I smiled, but there was nothing to it. I walked over to

the pond and dipped my toe into the clear edge. The ripples died only a foot away, swallowed by the thick green layer.

"Whatever," I said. "It was a stupid idea anyway."

"There are no stupid ideas," Aaron said. "Only nasty ponds with prehistoric algae."

He laughed, but I couldn't help feeling robbed. When was the last time we'd done something like this together? Something that wasn't with a bunch of his friends. We were so close, and it was frustrating to see it vanish that quickly.

"Let's just go back to the house."

Aaron clapped. "That's the best idea you've had all night, Abs."

I followed him back through the field, to our house. I expected him to open the door and end the night. But instead, he turned to me and said, "Commando time."

In one quick movement he was up the birch tree that hung over our patio and onto the roof of the house. The moon outlined him in a subtle white as he whispered down to me, "Are you coming or not?"

I climbed the tree, moving slowly until he was holding my hand and leading me to the middle of the house, where the roof peaked. I had no idea if he'd done it before, or if the idea came to him on the walk back from the pond. Either way, we sat there, our legs stretched over the rough shingles still warm from the day. Telling stories about Mom and Dad. Laughing, one-upping, and doing our best to keep from rolling off the steep roof as we watched the moon drop from the sky.

SIX

WE SNUCK INTO THE VAN, MY HEART STILL DOUBLED UP AND in my ears. Even when we were safe and wrapped in our blankets, I couldn't fall asleep. Aaron's words haunted me, though not because I thought he would actually leave. Instead, it was the truth of what he said. Mom and Dad have not tried to get us out once. We eat in churches and sleep in the van like it's normal. Like we will do this forever.

Thinking about it kept me up most of the night, and it's only when I wake up that I'm sure I've slept. For a few perfect seconds, with my head under the covers, I could be anywhere. I could be at home. My neck wouldn't ache from sleeping in a chair and everybody would be waiting for me to wake up, to come down for breakfast. If I can keep my eyes closed forever, maybe I won't have to feel the anxiety grip my stomach in its familiar cold hand.

When I pull the blanket away from my head, Dad is talking quietly with Mom. It only takes a minute for them to notice me listening. Mom reaches back like she wants to touch my leg.

"Did we wake you, honey?" she asks.

I shake my head, and even though I know they love us and wouldn't do anything to ruin that love, I can't shake it: We shouldn't be here. They should know.

"Gabs, it used to be you were the one waking us up," Dad says, leaning his head toward Mom. "Remember that, Kat?"

Mom nods. Dad watches me the same way he did when I was younger, like he can't believe how he ever got so lucky. I don't know why I can't open my mouth. Why I can't just say: *Do you see what's happening to us?* So when Dad turns back to me, I smile—hoping that maybe he'll see how fake it is. How hard I'm trying to pretend I'm okay, happy.

He doesn't.

"I was going to take a walk and grab a coffee," Dad says. "Feel like stretching those legs?"

✦ ✦ ✦

Dad walks just as fast as Aaron, but it's his long legs more than anything else. I am sore from yesterday, my body tight as I jog to keep up with him. When we were younger, Dad would go out to run almost every night, coming back with his T-shirt darkened by sweat. When he sees me pull up beside him, he stops and says, "Am I walking too fast?"

"No. I'm just trying to get loose."

Still, he slows down and I can tell it's killing him to move down the sidewalk at this pace. He nudges me in the shoulder and says, "Remember when we'd race in the parking lot of the mall? To the door?"

I still remember the first time I beat him, two years ago with Mom yelling behind us to watch the cars. But that mall was dead, like everything else in our town. All the big stores were gone, leaving behind a collection of flea market-style booths that were as aimless as the people who still shopped there.

"I remember blowing by you."

He huffs. "You beat me once, girl. And I think I was injured."

"Injured? Are you kidding me?"

He grabs his knee, moving it forward and back. “You know I’ve got a trick knee.”

“Well, anytime you want a rematch, old bones. Or should I say—old man.”

“Old man?” He shakes his head and then bends over into an awkward stretch, still talking to himself. “Old man.”

It surprises me how easily we’re able to fall back into the good-natured joking, as if we were walking through that same mall without a care in the world. And at the same time, it’s convicting. When did I let Aaron convince me that this familiarity was so easily lost?

“I’ll race you to the store,” I say. He probably won’t even be able to get out of the stretch he’s in, let alone run down the sidewalk with me. But then he’s gone, yelling “Go!” and moving faster than I thought he could.

I’m jumping off curbs, laughing as I chase him. Even with the head start, I’m beside him in less than a block. When he sees me pull up next to him, he pumps his arms even harder. But it’s pointless; I blow by him—past the restaurant on the corner, the men sitting in a circle at the park’s entrance, touching the store first, and easily.

When Dad finally shows up, all I can make out through the wheezing is: "Trick knee."

The grocery store is fancier than anything we had in North Carolina, full of organic this and fair-trade that. We never would have shopped at a place like this before, and the only reason we're here now is the free coffee.

Dad empties his third packet of sugar into the cup before saying, "I wanted to talk with you about last night."

At first my stomach flips, but I quickly realize he's talking about church—Brother John. He blows on his coffee and heads toward the aisles of food, looking at the shelves.

"I know this is confusing," he says. "But everything's going to be okay. I know it like I know the sun will rise. God's up there working right now, and all we have to do is wait."

He pulls a package of sugar-filled cereal from the shelf and looks at it. On a different day, in a different time, he'd be putting it in our cart and making me promise not to tell Mom. Hiding it behind boxes of crackers in the pantry. Stuff like that was always contraband in our house. But today he just puts it back on the shelf and starts walking again.

I try to forget what Aaron said last night, how we're never going home. How Dad and Mom have failed us. Instead I focus on racing Dad to the store. Putting that one carefree moment on a loop and playing it endlessly in my mind as a constant reminder that we haven't changed. Not really. Not ever. And maybe these glimmers of recognition are enough to start a fire—one that blazes high and hot enough that even Aaron can't ignore it.

I smile, and it's like Dad can see inside my head because he drains the cup of coffee and says, "So what are we going to do about that brother of yours?"

I could tell him what he wants to hear—that Aaron's fine. That we're all fine. All those white lies that fall from my lips so easily these days. But I don't.

"He's mad," I say. "Really mad."

"I know." He looks like he's been knocked to the ground as he says it. "But I also know that God still has your brother in his hands. He's going to be okay. We all are."

This is water on the fire—the only answer he gives anymore, and I hate it. Partially because I want to feel like we're not alone, that it's just a matter of believing more—believing better. But there's been so little proof. And even if that weren't the case, what are you supposed to do when every single day seems worse than the last? Are you supposed to keep pointing your head up and asking the same question over and over again?

It's so much easier than that, and he has to see it.

"What if we're not okay?" The question stops Dad cold. And once it comes from my mouth, I can't stop the other words from spilling out. "We could go home. That would make Aaron happy. That would make me happy. Can't we just go home?"

His face changes, the way it did when he came to school to tell me Grandma died. Like there weren't words to properly describe how he was feeling and no way to soften the blow.

"I know this is hard on you," he starts.

"If we go home, it won't be hard," I interrupt. "I know we don't have the house, but that's fine. We'll be fine."

"We can't leave, Gabs. Not now." Dad reaches out and hugs me in the middle of the store, but I don't even raise my arms. I become a statue.

I don't want to be mad at him, but how can he not see what's happening with Aaron, with all of us? He pulls me even closer, whispering in my ear—"God is working,

Gabs. Watching every step we take. We've got nothing to fear." We're standing there, still in the middle of the grocery store. I try to let myself get taken away by his words and his embrace. But nothing he says affects me at all. They're just words. Instead I watch the people moving slowly through the aisles, the only thing on their mind is the sort of chips they should buy. Whether it will be sandwiches or a salad for lunch. The injustice of it smacks me in the face, and all I want to do is run away, down the street screaming until I feel better. Until this makes sense. But Dad won't let me go, not even a little.

The first thing Dad says when we're outside is, "I'm not running anymore, so forget it." He laughs and walks a few steps ahead of me, his face lifted to the sky. I follow him, thinking about home and why that isn't good enough now. Even without the house, it makes more sense than this.

What's most frustrating is that it's not even a hard plan to imagine. We could call Uncle Jake and tell him we were coming home today and it would be automatic. We'd stay in his basement. Dad could get a new job. We would start over. That's how the story ends, or maybe how it begins. Either way, it's so obvious it makes my head hurt.

I don't realize we're standing in front of Brother John's building until Dad nods at the door and says, "Only a minute or two. Okay?"

He opens the door without waiting for my answer, holding it until I follow him into the dark building. The windows never let in enough light to make the room feel lit or warm, unlike the large stained glass of First Methodist, our home church. What light does slip in is neon from the liquor store across the street, making everything look as if it were on fire.

Dad is walking toward the front row of chairs when Brother John appears from his office.

"Oh, Brother John. I just though I'd take some time," he says, motioning to the cross. He seems so small whenever he's around Brother John, even though he's got six inches and at least fifty pounds on him. Brother John nods once, twice.

"Of course, Brother Dale. Maybe Abigail would like to come to my office while she waits? I just bought some muffins."

I grab Dad's hand, instinctively pulling myself closer to him. I don't want to sit and listen to Brother John for even a second, but Dad lets go of my hand and nudges me forward. I'm frozen, trying to figure out what I should do. Aaron wouldn't care. He'd walk for the doors right now, no matter what either of them thought. But I can't move. It doesn't help that my stomach rumbles like a car coming to life.

"A message from above," Brother John says, smiling.

His office is just as bare as the rest of the building. A Bible sits open on the desk along with a few newspapers. In the corner of the room, a large metal box rests on a card table. It hums softly, a pair of headphones and a large microphone beside it. Behind me, Brother John opens a box of muffins and puts one on a napkin for me.

"Have one," Brother John says, handing me a muffin. "They're fresh."

The muffin smells wonderful. I can almost feel the warmth trapped inside it. I imagine my teeth breaking through the crusty top. The soft sweetness of the middle.

"Go ahead. I'm sure you're hungry."

I take a small bite. It's carrot and close to divine. Brother John smiles, watching me eat, his hands folded. The second bite is just as unbelievable as the first. I don't say anything and neither does he until the muffin is nothing but crumbs. I pick them off the napkin, because I'm hungry and afraid of what I might say.

He finally breaks the silence. "How are you, Abigail?"

I don't know how to respond. Is it wrong to lie to a pastor? Is he really a pastor?

"Fine. Thank you."

Brother John nods and moves some papers across his desk. He motions for me to keep talking. I play with the napkin, twisting it into a cone. Every question I've ever had is rising up, and I'm doing my best to tamp them down. All I want to do is leave. For Dad to finish praying so we can get out of here.

"Well, I know this has been tough on you and your family," he says. "It's been tough on all of us. But what can you do? It's the Lord's world. He does with it as He pleases."

This annoys me, more than I'd like. It has been tough, even though that doesn't seem like the appropriate word. Disastrous. Cataclysmic. Apocalyptic—that one he'd surely like. But tough? It's been more than tough.

"I can tell you have something to say," he says. "Questions. Other things. I have questions, too. Know where I find the answers?"

He taps the Bible and smiles, waiting for me to say something. At first, I'm not going to say anything. I'll sit here, creating more and more awkward silence until Dad comes through the door. But then he says, "Everything happens for a reason."

And that's an answer I can't handle.

So, fine. He wants a question? A real question? I let him have the only one that any of us should be asking.

"Why didn't it happen?" I ask. I expect Brother John to get angry, to stand up and force me to repent right there. Instead he shifts back in his chair and runs his hands through his hair.

"I don't know. But I can assure you it was not God's fault. I must've gotten the date wrong. Or maybe we weren't ready yet. The important thing is that we remain steadfast in the Lord."

Of course this is the answer. It's been the answer ever since I knew there was a question. God is good and you do not question that goodness. Everything happens for a reason. We're supposed to sit down here waiting until God gets ready.

"I don't want to be here anymore," I say.

He doesn't seem surprised. He simply says, "Why?"

It's ridiculous, and I know my face shows my emotions like a mirror.

"Why? We're living in our van."

He nods, as if he's both tired of the conversation and has already heard the answer a hundred times before. The anger, the frustration—it's hot enough to burn through my skin.

"Sister, God's going to come down here and fix every problem this world has ever known. So keep that as your focus. If you remember God's plan, what you want becomes irrelevant."

I open my mouth, but Brother John holds up his hands.

"We all have to accept the situation God gives us and move forward humbly and fearfully. Anything less is obstinacy. It's sin, plain and simple."

I swallow once. "I don't know if I can do that."

Brother John stands up and comes around the desk. At first, I think he's going to try and hug me. Or maybe pray. Instead he kneels in front of me and says, "God never gives us anything we cannot handle. I want you to hold on to that whenever you start feeling doubtful. I want you to rest easy in the fact that God is doing all of this for a reason."

SEVEN

AS WE WALK BACK TO THE VAN, THE CONSTANT CLOUDS THAT pack the sky start to break up. Little beams of sunlight hit the ground. A few blocks later, the sky is clear. Dad doesn't speak as we follow street after street, a map he's surely memorized by now. His face is tired but focused, every bit of concentration going toward whatever is in his head.

I walk beside him, thinking about what Brother John said—this is happening for a reason.

Everything I've endured before has been small. Wearing hand-me-down clothing or not getting my license when everyone else was pulling into the school parking lot with their parents' truck. Growing up, Dad always told us that God took care of the birds and we were so much more to Him than a flock of birds. So whenever Mom came home with a new shirt or a pair of shoes, I counted it as proof that God was good, that he was watching over us every step of the way. But now I know those were small things, troubles that were easy to withstand.

I don't know what it says about me that I can't feel the same way about being here. That every minute we spend in this city pushes me further away from everything I want to believe. This could be a test and I'm failing spectacularly. But if it is? If God really is doing all of this for a reason, then I don't know what to think.

Because how does that make sense?

We turn a corner—the football stadium just in the distance—and a full blast of sunshine makes both of us shield our eyes. Dad says, "Well, look here. The sun shines in this place after all."

"I told Brother John I didn't want to be here anymore," I say. The words come out tentative, sheepish. "I'm scared. And I was happy when we didn't go. I was happy that all of us got in the van that night."

Just saying the words makes me feel lighter, and for a

second I think Dad is going to nod and tell me he feels the same way.

"I get scared too, Gabs."

If only he stopped right there.

"But God is up there watching everything we do, and when I get to thinking about that, all that fear drops away. All of it."

"Brother John said God is doing this to us," I say. "He says we're in the van for a reason."

Dad thinks for a second and then says, "Well, yeah. I mean, that has to be it, right? God is working—that does mean we're here for a reason. Doesn't it?"

Before I would've trusted him completely, would've pushed down all my questions and made whatever he said the infallible truth of my life. I search for even a flicker of that same trust now, but it's gone. We're thousands of miles from home—we'll shiver through another night in our van—and that should make him ask the same questions I can't escape. That should scare him enough that we aren't standing here talking about God.

I don't answer him and he must take the silence as agreement, because he puts an arm around my shoulder and says, "Hey, there's sunshine and we've got a good blanket in the van. What do you say we go down to that park and have ourselves a picnic? We'll even get that mopey brother of yours to come along. What do you think?"

I think: What will we eat and whose blanket will have grass all over it when we go to sleep tonight? Why are we having a picnic when we practically live outside? I want to grab him by the shoulders and scream: *Are you even paying attention?*

"Hey, c'mon, Gabs. Let's do this. It will be fun. Like the picnics we had at Baker's Mountain. Remember?"

He pushes my arm until I nod, pretending it's even close to the same thing.

Dad smiles big, bright. And as we start walking back to the van, I look up to the sky—squinting into the sun—and think: if You're really there, then help me.

We walk past kids with skinny pants and hats pulled low. Behind them are men with dogs and beards, laughing and passing around a bottle hidden inside a brown paper bag. The entrance to the park is full of people, all of them lying in the sun. Dad comments on everything as we walk down the hill toward a dark tunnel.

Aaron put up a huge fight about leaving the

van—especially when he heard we were coming to the park. Now Dad talks like it was Aaron's idea.

"Do you know anything about the park?" Dad asks Aaron, like he's some sort of expert on the city.

I expect him to ignore Dad, but he actually responds.

"It looks like a bunch of drug dealers and homeless people," Aaron says. "Really beautiful. I'm ecstatic."

I wince. Dad looks at Mom and says, "We should get him a job as a tour guide!"

Aaron doesn't smile. He walks ahead of us, looking around as if he expects somebody to jump out of the bushes with a knife.

For a second, the tunnel blocks out the sun. Dirt hangs from its top in unsteady cones and stagnant water collects along the sides. It feels like a place people get mugged. But when we reappear on the other side, the day is still nothing short of perfect. It's like fall in North Carolina, when you first start wearing jeans and a sweater. People are everywhere, thankful for the cloud break. Kids play. Some college-aged guys throw a football. Off in the corner a lady's dancing, her skirt flaring around her with each twirl.

Dad stops us in front of a patch of green grass and

Mom lays down a blanket. As soon as it's straight, Dad stretches his body across it and closes his eyes, basking in the sun. Mom begins unwrapping sandwiches, courtesy of the Baptists from two days ago.

"This is living," Dad says. "Good food. Good weather. My main squeeze, my favorite kids. It doesn't get better than this."

Mom smiles and puts a hand on his forearm before setting a sandwich on the blanket. Mom hands me one, too—bologna and American cheese—and I take a bite, dry as sand. Aaron hasn't touched his food or said a word to any of us. Even when I ask him if he wants to finish my sandwich, he just shakes his head and looks away.

I end up focusing on the playground, the kids climbing on something that looks like the sail of a ship. The more I watch, the more I wish I were younger. Slides and swings and sand—a paradise, once upon a time. Behind it all, kids scream as they use old pizza boxes to fly down a cement slide built into the side of a hill. Everybody seems perfect and happy.

"I'm going to go on the swings," I say.

"Take your brother," Dad says. "I could use some alone time with my lady."

Mom shakes her head, but smiles. I expect Aaron to roll his eyes, to sigh—something. Instead he's staring into the park nervously, as if he's ready to jump up and start running at a moment's notice.

"I don't want to go on the swings," Aaron says. "I want to go back to the van."

"He speaks!" Dad says. When Aaron doesn't respond, he says, "Go with your sister." When Aaron still doesn't say anything, Dad's voice loses the playfulness and all he says is, "Please?"

Aaron grabs his sandwich and stands up, walking directly for the swings without waiting for me. I'm trying to clean up my food when Mom touches me on the hand and says, "I'll get it. Go have fun with your brother."

I walk slowly, not sure if I want to be alone with Aaron right now. I know telling him anything that happened with Dad or Brother John will only solidify his anger, but the thought of keeping it inside—of living with it all by myself—is almost worse.

When I finally catch up with him, he's leaning against the swings, which are packed full of kids.

"Do you really want to swing?" he asks, looking across the park.

"It's better than sitting there doing nothing," I say.

He stands rigidly, annoyed with everything. If a kid walked by with an ice-cream cone, I swear Aaron would knock it out of his hands. And even though I have nothing to laugh about, the mental picture of that makes me smile.

"Well, I don't want to go on swings or get ice cream or go to the beach. I want to get the hell out of here. As soon as possible."

Behind Aaron comes the unmistakable sound of a trumpet. It doesn't take long for me to see the trumpet man outlined against the sky as he marches across the top of one of the park's rolling hills. He lifts the trumpet to his lips again and plays a note that sounds like a cow being strangled to death.

"Where were you guys anyway? You were gone forever," he says.

I hesitate, only a second.

"He took me to Brother John's."

That's when Aaron actually looks at me. Right in the eyes. "What? Why?"

"He wanted to pray." Aaron rolls his eyes and I continue, "So I had to sit in Brother John's office and talk with the man himself."

Aaron starts walking away from the swings, rubbing the back of his neck. "I bet that was a joy and a half."

If I tell him, it will be the end. I can see it on his face, the way his entire body is tensed and ready to fight.

"I asked him why the world didn't end."

Aaron stops walking. "You didn't."

I shrug. "He asked if I had any questions. Is there any other question you'd want to ask him? I mean, c'mon."

Aaron smiles, just barely. A sideways grin that I've seen too many times in my life. It's him calling BS.

"Yeah, right."

I raise my eyebrows, hoping the back and forth I know is coming will lift me above water. "I don't know what to tell you."

"Holy shit. What did he say?"

"That it was all a part of God's plan."

Aaron throws his hands up, the smile becoming strained. "Of course he did. Jesus. Of course that was the answer. Did anything else happen?"

It feels wrong keeping the rest from him. Racing Dad. How Aaron was right—we're not leaving. Everything Brother John said. But if I can avoid adding another log onto the fire of his resentment, I will. I'll do anything it takes to bring him back.

Just as I'm about to tell him I don't care about the swings, that we can go back to the blanket, a voice shouts, "Oh my God!"

At first I don't realize the girl—shocking red hair and clothes that look as if she got dressed in the dark—is talking to Aaron. Except she comes up behind him and wraps her arms around his body.

"Hey," he says, quietly and under his breath. Like he thinks I won't be able to hear. "Can we talk later?"

Slowly, a group of teenagers—their clothing mismatched and layered despite the warmth of the sun—materializes behind the girl. In the distance, another blast from the trumpet man rings out across the park.

"Who's this?" the girl asks. She's moved beside Aaron, her hand sliding into his. I can't stop staring at them.

Aaron mumbles my name and then adds, "She's my sister."

I expect a curled lip, or at least a raised eyebrow. And for a second, I think I might get both because the girl doesn't do anything except stare at me, wide-eyed like I was just dropped from the sky by a UFO. But then she lunges forward and hugs me. After the long, one-sided embrace, she turns around and hits Aaron hard on the chest.

"What the hell? You have a sister and not a single word?"

Her words gut me.

Aaron gives me this awful look, like I'm the one who shoved him into traffic. The girl is staring at me, too, but every time I try to say something I feel the words catch in my throat. All I can think about is how the world has expanded to include a possibility where Aaron occurs without me. And how do I even begin to verbalize that?

When he tells her we're twins, she nearly falls over.

"Twins? Are you shitting me?" She hits Aaron again. "Holy crap! You guys do look exactly alike!"

"Yeah, hence the whole twins part," one of the guys says from behind her. Aaron watches me as if he's trying to read my mind. I shoot warning messages to him: *Let's go. Now. Please.*

A few of the kids behind the girl laugh. At me? Or is it something else completely? Aaron shifts from one foot to the other.

"I'm Jess," the girl says to me. "And your brother is obviously an asshole. He has a sister and never said a damn thing!"

Something like that would normally make me bristle, the voodoo womb-loyalty kicking into fiery effect. But right now, she could say about anything and it wouldn't touch the anger—or maybe it's disappointment?—that's rising up inside me.

"Oh my God, you should totally come out with us tonight," Jess says.

Immediately Aaron says, "No."

"It's just Sea Cliff. We're not taking a midnight stroll in the Tenderloin. Jesus."

Jess turns to me and says, "It's a long walk, but that way we can get to know one another. Sound good?"

"She's not coming out," Aaron says. Jess responds with a single poke to his side, making him jump.

Jess turns to me. "Mr. Bossy Pants doesn't get a vote. So, what? You in?"

"I'm not being bossy, it's just—ah!"

Jess gets him in the ribs this time, grinning at me as she does it. I don't smile back. Everything about this girl is wrong. From her tangled hair, to her clothes, which haven't been washed in forever. Not to mention her friends, who look equally unclean and are laughing at everything she does. The only one who doesn't look positively thrilled is Aaron. Frustration is wrapped across his body like a rubber glove

"I want to leave," I tell Aaron. When he doesn't answer, Jess pokes him in the ribs and I can't help it. I turn on her. "Can you give us a minute? Please?" It comes out so nasty, I'm not sure who's more shocked—her or me.

"Yeah, sure. Listen, I was just—" Before she can finish, Aaron takes my wrist and walks a few steps away from the group. He bites the bottom of his lip for a few seconds before saying, "You're not going out with us tonight."

And despite all the other questions I want to ask him, the first thing that comes from my mouth is "Why not?"

He grimaces and looks back at Jess, who stands a few feet away from us with her hands on her hips. "I don't think it's a good idea."

"Well, here's something: I don't want to go with you." As soon as I say it, he brightens up. But then I say, "I don't want you going, either. You barely know these people, Aaron."

And I want to say: *What about me? Mom and Dad?* I didn't know why he was leaving, but knowing that it's just to come screw around with a bunch of homeless kids in the park makes me want to smack him in the back of the head.

It's another way we're falling apart, and he's doing it willingly. Before, at home, Aaron would never have snuck out. He didn't have to. But now, in this city, every time he leaves the van feels like desertion.

"C'mon, let's go back to Mom and Dad," he says, trying to push me forward.

"Is she why you're leaving?"

This stops him. "I don't want to talk about that now, Abs."

"Of course you don't."

Jess walks up to us cautiously, chewing her thumbnail and looking at Aaron. "Hey, it's not a big deal. I thought maybe she'd have fun. I didn't mean to start World War Three."

Aaron turns to her, his face annoyed. Tired. I don't care.

"It's not World War Three," he says.

"That's right," I say. "Because I'm coming."

Jess claps her hands. Behind her, a few of the guys raise their hands in the air jokingly. As if their team scored a goal, all of them seemingly thrilled. Except the one who matters, who looks like I just said the worst possible thing.

✦ ✦ ✦

Aaron doesn't seem angry until we're away from Jess and her friends, but then it covers his face like a new layer of skin.

"You're not going tonight. No way."

"Excuse me if I don't really respect your moral high ground," I say. "And it's not like you can stop me."

I don't know what makes me the maddest: him sneaking out to some homeless girlfriend, or how he thinks he can just tell me to be good and stay in the van while he's out doing—I don't even know what.

"I know," he says. "I can't."

"How inconvenient that you have a sister. Right?"

He looks down at his hands and then scratches his neck. The park is still bright and alive with people, but it all seems peripheral now.

"I was going to tell Jess about you."

"It must have slipped your mind while you were busy with all your new friends," I say.

The betrayal is more real than the air right now and the more I hold on to it, the more it feels alive inside me. But there's something else mixed in, a strange jealousy that I can't quite diagnose. It sits in my stomach, slowly pushing its way into my brain, where I can't stop wondering why he never asked me to come out with them—even if he knew I'd say no.

"Look, I was out and I met them once," Aaron says. "We hung out the next time. There isn't a lot happening at three in the morning. I'm sorry I didn't tell you."

I didn't realize how close we were to Mom and Dad. I can see them on the blanket. Mom is still lying down, but Dad is up and staring at us. He calls, "Well, look what the cat dragged in!" Aaron's eyes become fixed; the way he is when we're at Brother John's. Other than his feet, his body barely moves as we walk toward them. A slow metamorphosis from alive to barely living.

"If it's not a big deal, then why can't I come with you—and don't say Mom and Dad, because that's not it. I know it isn't."

Aaron waits for a moment before he says, "Because I knew you were going to act like this."

The objection comes to my lips quick, but I can't get it out. Act like this? I'm trying to keep us together and it annoys me that he doesn't see it. But at the same time, that jealousy bubbles up, and no matter what I do, I can't force it back down.

"I'm just worried about you."

"Yeah, you keep saying that. But did you ever think that I needed this, Abs?"

"Well, you could've brought me with you," I say. "Am I really that much of a loser that you can't let me meet your friends?"

"That's not it," he says quickly.

"Then tell me why."

He struggles for a second, looking at the ground. Finally he says, "I just needed something good, okay? And I knew that you wouldn't like it. I knew as soon as I even mentioned it, you would freak out."

"Because it's dangerous," I say.

"It's not like I'm out running guns for the Hells Angels, Abs! We hang out. We talk. It's a chance to get away, that's it."

"Sounds really wonderful," I say, trying to be sarcastic.

"You're proving my point. Right now. Even if I brought you on the very first night, we'd still be having this conversation."

Aaron looks over my shoulder, back to the hill where his friends are now sitting. I don't see or hear the trumpet man anymore. Aaron covers his face with a single hand, like he's trying to wipe away the past few minutes.

"You know what, whatever. I'm not going out tonight. You win."

Dad walks up behind Aaron and claps a hand on his shoulder, giving us both this big smile. I look at Dad and then back to Aaron, hoping to feel happy. Because didn't I just win?

But the only thing I feel is relief. And that's not the same thing. Not even close.

EIGHT

WHEN WE GET BACK TO THE VAN, DAD MOVES US TO A NEW spot—just a few blocks away from Brother John's church. Parking is by the hour in most places, and the meter maids dart around like flies in the summer, keeping time and waiting.

As soon as he turns off the engine, Dad closes his eyes—"Just for a bit," he says—and we sit there.

The sun is still shining and people walk past our van in groups, some of them looking at Dad sleeping against the window. The more I sit here, the more the relief from the park transforms into frustration. If Aaron was going out to spray-paint buildings, I would almost feel better. Because at least I could muster some real outrage. But wanting to be happy isn't wrong. It makes all the anger I've felt toward him in the last weeks seem petty. But at the same time, why can't he be happy here with us? Why does he have to go out and create something new?

Even if I asked, he probably wouldn't say a word. And that's the real problem. It's not him leaving, even though I hate it. It's him not talking. It's him sitting in the back of the van right now, pretending to read a book when he's got so much to say.

The van is too small. Too constricted. I feel like I can't breathe.

I lean up to Mom, almost asleep herself, and say, "I'm going for a run."

She rubs her eyes. "What?"

"I'll be careful," I say. "I need to get out of here for a bit, Mom. I promise I'll be back before dinner."

I don't ask. I don't even wait for her to answer. I'm pulling on my shoes and sweatshirt as she nods, her eyes already closed.

Aaron starts putting on his shoes, too.

"I want to go alone," I say. "I just need to get away. Sound familiar?"

"Yeah, okay. Whatever."

"I'm serious. I don't want you to go."

I open the side door and do a fast couple of stretches. Aaron jumps out and lifts his hands over his head, yawning.

"You're not going," I tell him.

"You can't stop me," he says. "Does that sound familiar?"

I hate him right now. His face. The way his words are like barbs in my skin. Everything. But I know he's going to follow me wherever I go, even if it's back to the van. And that's what I should do, if only to spite him. But now that I'm in the fresh air again, the thought of sitting in the stuffy van is worse than anything Aaron can say or do.

So I start walking, fast, and say, "Try to keep up."

Even when I start running, Aaron stays with me, stride for stride. I turn up a fairly gruesome hill, sure he'll quit and begin walking, but he actually pulls ahead of me. He's jogging in place when I finally make it to the top.

"You okay?" he asks, smirking.

I fly past him, faster than I should after that hill. But it feels good, if painful, to push myself. Aaron is behind me, his breathing growing heavier and heavier with every stride. A small victory.

The last time I heard him breathe that way was our first

night in San Francisco. Aaron was more nervous than I was. Our whole lives we'd been taught to be good, to do the right thing, so that when it came time to account for ourselves, we'd go up and not down. Take that elevator straight to heaven. I have no idea if that's what was going through his mind as Brother John stood up in front of us that first time, breathless and talking about the end of the world. But his usual bravado was muted, and he sat next to me the way he would when we were younger, as still as the sky after a storm.

"Abs, I need to stop." Aaron's voice is pinched as he speaks. I keep going, though, until he stops and says, "C'mon. I need a break."

I realize how tired I am once I stop moving. My legs wobble as I walk, trying to breathe. Aaron is a few steps behind me, and neither of us speak.

After that first night, Aaron went silent in every possible way. Whatever fear he showed was gone, and from that point on it was like looking at a beige wall. No emotion. No feelings. Nothing. It deteriorated more and more until he stopped talking almost completely. I was so worried about him—I am worried about him—but now I know it doesn't matter. Now I wonder if he saves everything for

Jess. For his nights away from all of us.

From the corner of my eye, I watch Aaron. He's got a hand on his side, but he's breathing regularly again. I start to jog. At first he doesn't join me, but then he starts moving. Slowly he pulls up next to me, and we jog back to the van without a word.

Brother John jumps around the front of the room as he speaks, his hands above his head like radio antennas receiving a signal. People "Amen" and "Praise the Lord" as he claps his hands together a few times. Soon the whole room is in rhythm.

"Here we come, Lord! Here we come!"

Aaron claps once, mocking them.

"That Holy Spirit is working tonight, yes sir. I can feel it in my blood, brothers and sisters!"

Feet stomp and chairs scrape the unpolished floor as voices climb the walls. Brother John stands at the front, taking it all in like oxygen.

"All you have to do is ask God for what you want! Just reach out and say, 'C'mon, Lord!'"

I try.

I search for the sprig of warmth in my stomach,

remembering how it would grow wildly, pushing into my arms and legs—everywhere—until it felt like, no matter what happened, God was listening.

When nothing happens, the tears come hard and violent.

Dad takes my hand; he's crying, too. But not for the same reason.

"Help Aaron."

"Help Mom and Dad."

"Help us figure this out."

I whisper all of these things, but it feels like knocking on the door of an empty house. The only sound is my fist against the hard wood, the way it echoes through the rooms before finally disappearing.

This can't be your plan.

I'm tired of sleeping in our van, of not having enough of anything. Of losing my parents to this. My brother.

Please.

Around me, the room moves as people dance and sing and pray. Brother John shouts over all of it, dancing, too—gripped by the Spirit. And then he falls, pitching forward right beside me. It's instinct that makes me reach out and catch him.

The room gasps. Brother John trembles in my hands, moving like a caught fish. Like he just got plugged in. People stand up and circle around us, still dancing and singing and praying. No one helps, even as his dead weight almost brings me to the floor.

Brother John shivers again, and when he speaks it's not words—more of a babbling that rises and falls from his lips. Like a toddler learning to speak.

I can smell him, sweat and fast food. He grunts as if he's the one trying to hold somebody up. The more he writhes, the more my hands begin to cramp. Finally Dad takes Brother John by the other arm, helping me lift him up.

The crowd of people has circled around us now, all of them hungry with expectation. Their prayers fill the room. Every face is turned up to the ceiling, every body coming closer and closer—choking me with their movement, their noise. I try to focus on Brother John, infused with a spiritual gravity intent on bringing him to the floor.

Dad's eyes are closed and he's praying, one hand lifted in the air while Brother John's blathering gets louder. People reach toward us, their eyes glassy with tears. I search for Mom, for Aaron, but they're lost in the crowd, faceless. Heat seems to blow through the floor, the walls. The room blurs around the edges.

The voices of the crowd lift higher. Hands reach up, like people drowning in water. Like somebody will reach down and pull them up for air.

A woman falls to the ground. A man begins to dance, kicking his body around in circles. Hold on. Hold on. Don't drop him. But everything is twisting together. The sounds. The colors. The faces of the people, dancing and screaming right in front of me.

Brother John's body jerks forward; my hands slip.

From far away the sound of a drum beats in my ears, my chest. It gets faster and faster until it's the only thing I can hear. And then something swims toward me. It's Aaron's face. His hand reaches out for me and then it's the floor and the sense I'm flying. Is it finally happening? Is this what it feels like?

When I open my eyes, Mom and Dad are above me. Brother John has his hands in the air.

"Here is a daughter of the Lord!"

Mom leans close to me and says, "Abigail, are you okay?"

I feel thick and my mouth is dry. Dad's eyes are alive with excitement; he reaches down and helps lift me to my feet. I'm unsteady, but I don't feel as if I'm going to pass out again.

Brother John puts a hand on my shoulder as he says, "When you ask for a message, God delivers. Sister Abigail's had a heavy heart. She had questions—we talked about them just this morning. So God said, 'Listen, now. I'm about to give you an answer. I'm going to give you some of that Holy Spirit.'"

Everybody nods, whispers "Amen." I search the room for Aaron, finding him in the back—alone and looking like he's the one who passed out. Everybody else is focused on Brother John.

"You heard me," Brother John says. "God gave me a message for you. But if you needed more proof, look at Sister Abigail. That's God getting your attention. He wants to make sure you hear this message."

The serenity of the room dissolves and people are on their feet once again, yelling for Brother John to tell them more—to give them the message. Brother John smiles, raising his hand for silence.

"Brothers and sisters, you already know. God is calling us home. He's calling us home."

The room explodes with movement, excited voices. Dad grabs Mom and pulls her to him, tears rolling down his face. Brother John puts both hands on my shoulders again as he says, "The only question is: Are you ready? Because we're all going to see the Lord very soon. Amen?"

The whole room says it—"Amen."

One loud, corporate agreement. Nobody notices when I don't move my lips.

NINE

I DIDN'T THINK IT WAS POSSIBLE FOR THE VAN TO BE QUIETER than it's been the last few days, but it is now. Aaron doesn't move, won't make eye contact. When we finally park, he buries himself in his sleeping bag and, presumably, falls asleep immediately. Dad, however, keeps looking back to me, and I know he wants to say something. It's as if he can't see past me into the backseat.

As we left the church, people stared like I'd penned an addition to the Bible. Brother John paraded me around the room, telling everyone to be ready. That God has spoken.

All I want to do is sleep, but I can't. Every time I close my eyes, I'm flooded with images of Aaron's face. With the sound of Brother John's voice as he said, "Be ready,

Brother Dale. I wouldn't be surprised if God came for us this week!" Nobody was happier in that room than Dad. Not a single person.

"Hey, Gabs." Dad leans toward me so he won't wake up Mom or Aaron. He looks almost jubilant. "What was it like? Hearing God's voice."

Do I tell him I heard Mozart? Saw winged cherubs with harps in flowing gowns of white? Gold streets? Saw Grandpa and Grandma and felt the fullness and the peace of standing in front of God? Anything other than what I know really happened: All I ate today was a banana, a muffin, and a few bites of bologna sandwich and then I ran—how many miles? Too many, I guess.

I always wanted to believe God cares about us, that all the praying and dancing and singing actually works. I wanted to believe that God can come down here and knock somebody out like a prizefighter, just to get our attention. I understand Dad's need like it's my own, because it always has been.

But the truth is, nothing happened. I asked—I begged for it—and God didn't do a thing. Telling him that would break him. But if I lie, we'll never leave.

"Do you feel different?" he asks.

I take a breath, just a sip of air, and decide on a third way.

"Can we go home now?"

Dad seems surprised. For a few seconds, as I'm staring into his eyes—the darkness of the van shadowing half of his face—I let myself believe he will say yes. I imagine yelling for Aaron, for Mom—seeing the excitement in their faces. Nestling into my seat as the lights of the city slowly dissolve behind us.

But I know better. And when he stumbles over his words, it's all the confirmation I need.

"Oh, Gabs. Hey—I mean. Well. We're so close now."

The worst part is: he can't believe I'd even ask. Us leaving—saying no to Brother John, to this city—is so impossible to comprehend, that the only response is astonishment. His face, those words, they finish me off. Aaron moves in his sleeping bag, and I hope he can't hear this. I hope he's actually asleep.

"You heard Brother John. It's happening."

Whatever I think—yes, no—doesn't really matter. Dad isn't listening to what I'm saying anymore, just like God. They're both preprogrammed to a default setting, running forward blindly.

"Dale," Mom says from the front seat. I didn't know she was awake. Her voice is soft, like so many times from our childhood. Dad turns to her. "Tomorrow, okay?"

Dad nods and I pull the blanket over my head. I don't want him to see me crying. I wrap myself in the quilt and try to fall asleep as quickly as Aaron convinces Mom and Dad he does.

I almost scream when Aaron touches my shoulder, his face close to mine. His mouth is right in my ear.

"Quiet," he says. He hands me my hooded sweatshirt. "Come outside."

"What's going on?" I whisper, pulling it over my head. But Aaron shakes his head and silently steps to the back seat, undoing the window and then the door. He drops the bungee cord, and it rattles against the side of the van. We both look at Mom and Dad. Neither moves. Aaron tosses a hat to me before slipping outside.

Cold air spins around the van and, for a second, I'm dizzy. Through the open door Aaron is watching me. I put up my hood and climb over the backseat, joining him on the street.

He closes the door quickly and then takes my hand and

pulls me down the block. We're fifteen feet away from the van when I stop him.

"What are we doing?"

"Going to meet Jess," he says. At her name, I draw back. "Abs, c'mon."

"I thought you weren't going," I say.

"Well, things change."

"I'm going back to the van," I say, wrestling my arm away from him.

But it's an empty threat, because I don't move. We stand there, the cold settling on me like a sickness. Aaron kicks at a streetlight, frustrated. I blow into my hands. Somewhere in the darkness, a car horn sounds.

"If it makes any difference, I wasn't planning on coming out tonight," Aaron says. "I was going to keep my promise. But then you went all evangelist on me."

I bounce up and down, trying to generate some heat.

"I didn't go evangelist. I don't even know what that means."

"It means I thought you became one of them. Got slain in the spirit, or whatever."

I stare at him. He looks genuinely worried. "Don't worry. God definitely didn't say anything to me. I barely ate all day, and it was really hot in there. That's it."

Aaron nods slowly, searching my face. "Okay. Still. Come out with me tonight. Get to know Jess."

I shake my head. I don't see any reason to get to know her. The only reason I wanted to go before is because he didn't want me to. Now, all I can think about is my quilt.

"I'm the judgmental jerk, remember? You were really worried about that before."

"Oh, please. I know you're not still mad about that," he says, waving my words away with a quick movement of his hand. "Quick quiz: Do you hate being stuck in that van? Do you like fun? If the answer to either of those is yes, and I know they are, then let's go. Because, fun ahead, Abs. Fun ahead!"

I can't tell if he's mocking me, a tactic that usually works. And he might be, but there's something different about him. He suddenly seems unburdened, as if some invisible weight has been lifted off of him. I would give anything to shed everything I'm worried about, even for a few hours—a night. I have to look away from him. I shake my head for good measure.

"If you hate it, we can leave."

He smiles, so big. So real. So him.

It scares me how unsure I am right now. How tempted I am to go with him, even though I know it's wrong. But more so, I'm scared that being out here with Aaron might change me in the way it's seemed to transform him. To trim away whatever is left of who I used to be.

We walk to a part of the city I don't know, full of Chinese restaurants and other shops that are all closed. As soon as Jess sees us, she comes running. I don't know what to do or say, especially when she puts her arm around my shoulder and announces, "Okay, Sea Cliff awaits!"

Jess and her friends lead us through the streets of San Francisco like they own it. And they might as well. The street stretches out before us, empty but strangely wonderful. Christmas lights—still up—brighten otherwise dark storefronts, making the entire road feel festive. I focus on this and not the people sleeping in the corners of the dark buildings we pass, trying not to worry about how long it will take for us to get to these cliffs, or how Jess is holding Aaron's hand and whispering into his ear every few steps.

Every person in the group talks loudly and, it seems, to every other person in the group no matter who they're actually addressing. I don't say a word, even when Aaron looks over at me and asks, "You doing okay?"

"Of course she's okay. It's a beautiful night with beautiful scenery." Jess waves toward a window filled with dead ducks hanging from hooks. "And, of course, great company."

One of the others, a small and dirty boy with dark blond hair, kisses her on the cheek as she says it. Aaron laughs with the rest of them, putting his arm around Jess and saying, "Okay, calm down now. . . ."

When the same boy comes next to me, looking like he might try it again, I take a few quick steps forward and find myself next to the only other girl in the group, besides Jess. She has short hair—she could easily be mistaken for a boy—and wears what look like ski pants. She doesn't say anything to me, but it doesn't seem like she wants to kiss me, either, which is a preferred quality. We walk for blocks and blocks this way, listening to everyone else talk and sing and laugh. I can't help but look back every time I hear Aaron's voice.

I've never seen Aaron act this way around a girl. He hangs on every word and he hasn't stopping smiling since we met up with Jess. When she trips on a broken piece of cement, Aaron catches her and they hold on to each other for three whole blocks.

We slowly wind our way into a more residential area, filled with identical houses that seem stuck together in one long row. That lasts for more blocks than I can count. I don't hear the ocean, and the thought of a cliff being anywhere close to these houses seems improbable. But then the world opens up and I stop walking, shocked.

"This is Sea Cliff?" I ask.

Large houses—mansions, basically—glow all around us. These are houses with maids and great rooms, the sort of houses you see on television. Ahead, the street twists in and around with no discernible landmarks.

"What did you expect?" Kissing Boy asks.

"I don't know. Woods? Animals?"

One of the boys—he has dreadlocks that hang down to his waist—laughs and says, "The only wildlife out here are the Jaguars parked in the driveways."

The girl with the ski pants adds, "Yeah, not that kind of cliff."

The deeper into the neighborhood we go, the quieter and quieter the group gets. As if we might wake up one of these giant houses. My mind comes alive with possible explanations, all of them involving police and us having to run away. Aaron still has his arm around Jess—they could be walking around the mall together and it wouldn't look any different. But I can't help myself. I walk up to him and try to talk as quietly as I can.

"I'm not robbing anybody," I say.

"What? That's not what this is, Abs."

Jess steps away from Aaron and says, "Oh, Jesus." Her voice carries, so everyone can hear. "No, no. We're not going to rob anybody."

I'm hot with embarrassment, enough that I don't want to say anything else. Everybody is watching me, their faces hidden by shadows.

Aaron comes over to me and says, "There's a beach down here. That's where we're going."

"And why the hell would you think we were going to rob somebody?" One of the boys, wearing a bandana over his short red hair looks offended. "That shit's racist."

Dreadlock Guy says, "Dude, you're white. How in the hell is that racist?"

Bandana Kid thinks for a second and then says, "This chick shows up and thinks we're going to start stealing? It might not be racist, but it's definitely not cool."

Aaron looks embarrassed. It should make me feel at home, because this is who I've always been. Abigail, Aaron's uptight sister.

Dreadlock Guy says, "Hold up, Jordy. Didn't you get busted for larceny? Like, two weeks ago?"

This fact is met by a collective "Ohhhh!" and Bandana Kid curls his lip and gives his friend—and me—the finger.

"I'm just saying. Shit's prototypical, that's all."

"Jesus. The word is *stereotypical*, you idiot," Dreadlock Guy says, turning to look at me with an apologetic smile.

"This is my fault," Jess says to me. "I thought it would be a surprise. I thought it might be something you haven't done yet. Because, you know." She twirls her hand around the neighborhood, taking in all the mansions with a single swipe. "It's not like people like us are welcome here in rich-bitch country."

While the rest of them debate the other places we could've gone, I focus in on three words: "people like us." I look at the group. One of them has pulled out a small cigarette, the smoke rising slowly into the night. Their hair is long and stringy, their faces thin and red from constant exposure.

We might be the same age, even have some favorite

movies or books in common. We might be stuck in San Francisco right now. But Aaron and I aren't here forever. We didn't choose to skip school and live in the park. This is temporary, and that makes us different in a fundamental way.

"I shouldn't have assumed," I say.

Jess puts her hand on my arm and says, "Really. It's cool. Jordy is one of those activist kids. Always outraged about something."

I'm about to apologize again when Kissing Boy says, "Okay, this is great and all, but can we please get the hell off the street before somebody sees us and really decides to call the cops? I don't feel like spending the night in jail."

"But you met that nice man last time," Jordy says. "The one who wanted to take your picture."

"Nah, that was E," Kissing Boy says, slapping the dreadlocked boy on the butt. "Look how pretty he is."

"It was only once. And he said he loved me," E says. "Don't judge, man."

Everybody laughs and this time I join them—cautiously at first. I catch Aaron watching me and I cock an eyebrow like, *What? It's funny, right?* But this time Jess is the one telling people to shut up.

"Seriously," she says. "I don't want to deal with the cops tonight."

I must still look horrified, because Jess says, "They've only called the cops once or twice. But we were being stupid, so . . ."

It doesn't make me feel better. Suddenly, the night feels darker, colder. The paranoia comes heavy, like a fog. What am I doing out here with these people? Fun for me never involved the threat of police.

Jess smiles, almost embarrassed.

"You're going to like it. Trust me."

"We could go back to the park," Aaron offers. Jordy boos and Jess cocks her head to the side, surprised. But he wants to go with them—with Jess. It's so obvious. He has one foot already in the direction everybody else has started to walk, and I don't want to disappoint him.

"We came all this way," I say, shrugging.

Jess claps her hands once and kisses Aaron, and I look away, catching up with the group as they lead us along more of the same nondescript roads that brought us this far into the neighborhood.

Jess walks casually, as if she were going to her house. As if she didn't just have a face full of my brother. I can tell

Aaron is embarrassed, walking with his arms straight at his sides. It's not until Jess wraps an arm around his waist that he actually begins to look normal again.

Everybody stops in front of a tall chain-link fence. Behind it, in the darkness, waves crash against rocks. Salt fills my nose, the smell transforming into memories of me and Aaron playing on the beach, our legs raw from the sand and our backs hot from the sun. Myrtle Beach in the summer, Dad's unnatural ability to find the worst motel no matter how many times we made the trip—all of it rushes over me like one of those warm ocean waves.

I'm not sure if I'm relieved or disappointed that the fence is locked and looped with thick chains.

"It's closed," I say. A few of the kids laugh, and Jess puts her foot onto the chain link, pulling herself up.

"Only for the mortals, Abs," she says, climbing up and over the fence in only a few movements. The others follow until it's only me and Aaron standing there.

"Can you get over it?" he asks.

"Of course I can get over it," I say. "What kind of question is that?"

But I don't hop the fence with the rest of them because that's not what's bothering me. "She called me Abs."

He shrugs. "Is that a bad thing?"

It's familiarity. Only Aaron has ever called me it—because when we were little, he stuttered and couldn't get Abigail to come off his tongue. Right or wrong, it was always ours—mine. And hearing Jess say it bothers me, even if I can't fully say why.

Jess rattles the fence and says, "You guys coming?"

Aaron looks at me before putting his foot into the fence. I don't have much of a choice but to follow him, and when my feet are on the sandy pavement on the other side, he smiles and points to a dark wooden staircase. The others, except for Jess, have already started down.

"Be careful. It's super dark," Jess says.

As we take the steps down toward the beach, the fog thickens and the sound of waves crashing against the rocks comes again from the darkness. Below us, on the beach, the others are running and yelling, shapeless shadows that disappear into the darkness like tiny ghosts.

I turn in their direction, and Jess stops me. "We'll go down there in a minute. I want you to see something first."

She goes the opposite way, leading us to a second staircase, which ends in front of a huge boulder. In the darkness, my feet find grooves cut into the rock by the wind and the sand, perfect steps. As I put my foot in the first one, Jess's hand appears above me. She pulls me to the top of the boulder, where the entire bay spreads out beneath us. In the distance, the fuzzy lights of the Golden Gate Bridge fight to break through the thick air.

We stand there, staring at the bridge and the fog, as Aaron climbs up and stands between us.

"I love this," he says.

Even through the fog, the bridge seems alive, bigger than anything I've ever seen. Lights from distant cars skip across it before disappearing into the darkness on the other side. I want to know what's out there, where it takes people. But I don't ask, only watch. I could sit here all night.

"This is one of the first places I found when I came to the city," Jess says. "I thought it was my own little secret. Like nobody ever noticed this perfect beach. Or the staircase, for that matter."

She laughs.

"I was stupid. About a lot of things."

Aaron puts his arm around her and she leans her head onto his shoulder, still talking.

"For a long time, this was the only place I felt safe. I'd sleep down on the beach, next to another boulder. Even now, if things get too crazy, I come down here."

Jess smiles but it reminds me of Mom—a flare that burns bright, only to go out just as quickly. In front of us, the bridge sits in its hazy glory, oblivious to anything other than itself.

"Do you still sleep here?" I ask, wondering if Aaron walks her all the way out here every night. Would he do that for her? It seems like him.

"No. It's . . . well, it's just not as hidden as it used to be, I guess."

I look around. Up on this boulder, you wouldn't be able to see us from the parking lot above. It does feel safe. A place to get lost.

Down on the beach, the others are yelling for us to come down—"Get off that damn rock and play with us," a guy—maybe E—shouts. Jess and Aaron share a look and a smile before Aaron says, "You're going to love this."

The beach is dark and magical, the bridge hanging over us like something from a dream. A group of shadows—the others—collect near the water's edge. As we get closer, the shadows resolve into more familiar outlines. Dreadlocked E, the girl with the ski pants, Kissing Boy. Jordy the

Activist. They all stand a few feet away from the water, hanging on one another's shoulders and laughing. When a wave comes rushing back into the beach, they run toward us, laughing even louder.

"It's kind of a game," Jess says. She seems embarrassed by it, as if Aaron and I are sitting in the van playing video games and watching movies. Kissing Boy runs up to us, grabbing Jess by the arm and pulling her down toward the water. As they disappear into the dark, he says, "The only rule is: Don't get wet!"

"Or hypothermia!" somebody else yells.

"It's weird," Aaron says. "But fun."

They yell for Aaron and then—I don't know why I'm surprised—me.

"You can wait up here if you want," he says. But I don't answer him. I go running into the dark, toward the voices calling my name, smiling even though none of them can see me. I don't see the water and almost go headfirst into a wave. E catches me and says, "Whoa. I know you're excited, but slow down there, Captain. We don't want you falling in yet."

The rules are simple, they explain. When the tide retreats, everyone has to run around a large rock that gets swallowed up as soon as the water comes surging back toward us. If you get wet—"And wet is a relative idea," E says. "Because, really, everybody gets wet."—you are out.

"It gets harder because, you know, the tide isn't going to stop coming in," Kissing Boy says. "And it's crazy dark."

I take off my shoes, trying not to hear Mom's voice in my head—worried about riptides and sharks. I try to be carefree, like them, and not worry about what could happen. So when the water pulls back from the shore, I run as fast as I can—the sand cold on my feet—and make it back around the rock before any of them. I'm breathing hard from the cold, the rush of it all.

"Holy shit, did you see that?" E, who slipped and fell just as the tide was coming back, is soaked but wide-eyed with surprise. "Are you kidding me?"

"I'm surprised she didn't ask us to put money on it," Kissing Boy says, equally wet and amazed. When E fell down, he grabbed the other boy's leg. "And I'd also like to file a formal complaint against this asshole."

"The only rule is: Don't get wet," Jess says. "You're usually pretty adamant about that, Silas."

Silas and E stand aside as we line up and wait for the next waves to pass. It's Aaron, me, Jess, and the girl in the ski pants, whose name is Laina, I learn. Just as the water crashes into the rock, I go—maybe a bit too early but by the time I'm on the ocean side of the rock, the water is already a foot down the beach. I make it back before both Jess and Aaron. When I see Jess, she's drenched and pushing Aaron—bone-dry—who's laughing. Laina never left the starting spot. She's sitting with E, Jordy, and Silas saying, "I've got to sleep outside tonight so this suddenly seems really stupid."

When Aaron and Jess get back to us, Jess is trying to act mad. I know the feeling so well, it could be my own. Aaron, as always, plays the innocent. "What? I can't help it you tripped."

"Whatever. That's some cheating mess," Jess says. She looks at me and says, "Listen, kick your brother's ass for me, okay?"

She lifts her fist for me to bump, nodding and smiling. I meet it weakly and try to smile, too. For some reason, when Aaron sees this, he cracks up.

"What?" Jess says.

Aaron shakes his head, still laughing. "Oh, nothing."

But then he lifts up a hesitant fist for E to bump, both of them dying with laughter at the dainty exchange.

"Okay," Jess says to me, "now I really want you to kick his ass."

Aaron grabs Jess and tries to lift her off the ground. She screams, coming behind me for protection. Aaron's eyes are so bright, enough that I could probably see them from a hundred feet away, as he chases her. When he's finally got his arms around her, they both smile—lost for a second. Then Jess rushes away from him, laughing.

"That smooth shit isn't going to work for you tonight," she says. "It's payback time."

Aaron laughs.

"I'm going to let you guys in on a little secret: Abs here was born second. Like, literally. I'm older by two minutes, and she's never beaten me at anything in her life."

Again with the collective "Ohhh!"

Silas says, "You going to take that? Smoke his ass!"

Jess begins rubbing my shoulders like a boxing trainer and I'm watching the water, ignoring Aaron, who keeps reaching over to grab my arm. Trying to get whatever advantage he can. As soon as the water crests over the top of the rock, I'm going to run as fast as I can.

Just before it happens, Aaron leans next to me and says, "I told you this would be fun."

TEN

E LETS ME WEAR HIS COAT—WHICH IS MASSIVE—AS WE WALK back to the park. Aaron swaggers triumphantly at the front of the group.

"I mean, she's my sister," he says. "But if you try to take a man's crown, there are consequences."

"Some man," Jess says. "You totally pushed her—and me."

Aaron looks offended. "Don't be a sore loser. Abs, tell them I didn't push you."

I'm so cold I can barely talk without my teeth sounding like a machine. Jess stands right next to me, so close our arms brush every few steps. If she's cold, I can't tell. She walks tall, fast.

"Look at your poor sister. She's going to freeze, and for

what? So you can be a big man winning all the games?"

Jess is kidding, but the truth of the statement stops Aaron for a moment. Like, Oh yeah, we don't have clothes or a way to dry them, anything. He could be Mom in the moment, the way anxiety crawls across his face. Before Jess or I can say anything, Silas says, "This boy's trying to kill his sister and his girlfriend!"

Ohhh!

I don't know who's more embarrassed, me or Jess. Her face is red and she won't look at me—anyone—as E and Silas push Aaron, who smiles and tells them to shut up. When I do make eye contact with Jess, all the confidence she's built up is gone. All she says is, "Boys . . ."

There were always girls who were interested, but I think Aaron was too embarrassed to bring them to our house. Sometimes they'd come up to me, asking questions. Maybe they'd go to a movie, or one of the school dances. Whether it took days or weeks, the girls always faded away, and when I'd ask Aaron all he'd say is, "You know how it goes, Abs."

But how does a girlfriend work out here? It's not like they can go on dates or come over to the van to watch a movie.

Aaron doesn't say much else as we walk. His smile is Christmas. It's us getting up ridiculously early and running down the hall, yelling until Mom and Dad got out of bed. Silas tells us how—when he was in school back in Oregon—there was this one girl he liked.

"I asked her out twenty times and she never said yes," he says. "I used to think it was funny, but now it's kind of depressing."

He turns to Laina, smiling. Before he can say anything she says, "No way. Look in a different direction."

This lightens the mood, but soon Aaron and Jess are walking behind the rest of the group. I try not to eavesdrop and to listen to what Silas and E are saying—asking Jordy about a music store near the park that supposedly still pays money for used CDs. But when Jess laughs, I glance over my shoulder. She's rolling her eyes and he's grinning. They walk shoulder to shoulder, their bodies bumping every few steps. Aaron leans over and quickly tries to kiss Jess on the cheek, instead getting her on the nose. They both laugh. As far as they're concerned, the rest of us don't exist. They're all alone in the world.

We enter the park in a place I've never seen. It's darker here, and I have to pay attention to every step I take. We don't follow the path, instead walking through the trees until we come out onto a long patch of grass. There are four or five other people already here, sitting against the same overstuffed backpacks everybody carries. Two scruffy dogs lay asleep next to a small tree.

"Will you look at this?" A voice stretches above the murmur. A tall, lanky guy, older than everyone else in the group by at least five years, slaps E on the shoulder and says, "That's right, the prodigal son has returned."

The guy gives me a once-over as he talks. Somebody calls him Skeetch, and he nods at them. But then it's right back to me, my skin crawling every time his eyes pass up and down my body. He juts his chin in my direction and says, "Who's the new one?"

E turns around. "Oh, that's Aaron's sister. They're from North Carolina."

"A southern girl?" Skeetch says. "I spent some time in Alabama back in the day."

Silas deadpans, "More like did some time."

Skeetch laughs, but it isn't friendly. His eyes are cold razors that cut from one person to the next. When Aaron and Jess appear from the trees he smiles, and it's as harsh as the bay wind.

"Well, well, well. Look at you," he says to Jess. "So, are you going to introduce me to your new friend?"

He reaches out to touch her arm, and she jumps back. "Don't touch me."

"Okay, okay," he says, raising his palms up. "Just saying hello. And it's not like I haven't before."

Aaron's face has transformed, gone from soft to hard as he eyes Skeetch, keeping Jess close to him.

"Maybe she doesn't want to say hello," Aaron says.

Skeetch laughs and says, "Maybe she doesn't want to say hello. Okay, tough guy. You keep telling yourself that."

E steps up to them and says to Skeetch, "Why don't we fire one up. Help everybody chill out. I know you're holding, man."

Skeetch doesn't say anything for a long minute, only stares at Aaron and Jess. His face is angular and hard, and even when he smiles there's a severity that doesn't go away. Nobody moves until he reaches into his coat and pulls out a small baggie, handing it to E.

"Whatever. Been there, done that, you know? Besides, I'm always open for new opportunities."

Skeetch sidles up next to me and Aaron steps between

us, putting one hand against his chest and saying, "Back off. Seriously."

E lifts up the bag for us to see and says, "Okay, now. Let's not ruin a good night trying to figure out which one of you is the bigger asshole."

Jordy is the only one who laughs.

"Too late for that," Jess says, trying to pull Aaron away. He won't move. Aaron and Skeetch stand a foot away from each other, eyes locked. Jess curses under her breath and leans close, saying something in his ear. When he finally moves, Skeetch laughs. "Well, I'd rather be the bigger asshole than the bigger bitch."

I can't tell who's laughing and who's not.

Jess doesn't stop moving until we're at the entrance of the park. Then she turns around and pushes Aaron.

"What the hell?"

"What am I supposed to do? Let him talk that way about you? About Abs? Hell no."

Jess shakes her head, but she doesn't disagree with him. "You walk away. No matter what happens, you swallow that macho bullshit and walk away."

"Are you serious?" Aaron asks.

Jess turns to me. All the playfulness from before is gone

when she says, "If he's not going to listen to me, then you need to. That asshole? He's nothing but a black hole. And if you're smart, you and your brother will stay away from him."

When she turns to go back to the park, Aaron steps in front of her and puts his hands on her shoulders and says, "Hey, hey—I'm sorry.

"Whatever. I need to get my stuff."

"Leave it. I'm sure E will take care of it."

"Oh, so you're the experienced street kid now? My stuff will be gone in a matter of minutes if I don't get it. And unlike you, I don't have a van and parents to escape to whenever I want."

Aaron flinches and Jess steps around him, getting about ten feet before he stops her again. From the road, I catch only small parts of their conversation, words like *Please* and *I can't* that lift above the noises of the city. Eventually Jess shakes her head and pushes Aaron away one last time before walking back into the darkness of the park.

When he sees me, Aaron doesn't say anything except, "Let's go."

I know he's going back out. That's why we're walking so fast, why he won't look at me. A month ago, I would've made deals with God to keep him in the van—offering promise after promise. But when we get to a familiar stoplight and I can see the van poking out of the haze just a few blocks ahead, I'm too tired to keep asking for help that never comes.

I can see Dad still slumped against the driver's side window. Mom's head is buried in a hat and covered by a quilt. We walk silently toward them, each step raising a conflict deep inside me. I don't want him to leave, but the thought of Jess being alone in the park with that guy gnaws at any selfishness I'm trying to hold on to.

As Aaron begins to undo the bungee cord, I stop his hand.

"Bring Jess back to the van."

Aaron turns around, the bungee cord still in his hand. For the first time in weeks, he looks surprised. "Yeah, right."

He tries to open the door to the van, but I block him. "Seriously. You're obviously worried about her. So why not?"

"If you have to ask that question, then you haven't been paying attention for, like, ever."

He tries to move me out of the way, but I'm not getting

in the van until he answers me. I have no idea what Mom and Dad would say if Aaron showed up with some homeless girl. But they'd have to say something. They'd have to do something.

"What are they going to say?"

"Oh, let's see. Dad will tell me Jess isn't part of God's plan. Because who needs a girlfriend when Jesus is coming back? You know."

He closes his eyes and drops his head. The silence is almost complete, except for a car alarm going off somewhere deeper in the city.

"So, she's your girlfriend."

He sighs, looking at the bungee cord in his hand. Then it's as if everything he's been holding back comes rushing out of his mouth.

"I have no idea if she's my girlfriend. It's not like we're going out on dates or sneaking off to make out in the bathroom during lunch."

"Okay, gross."

Aaron doesn't stop, though. "And if I thought I could bring her back here, I would. But this isn't any better. Not really." He stops, staring at me for a second before motioning to the van and saying, "I know you don't like it, but I need to make sure she's okay. Like, now."

"You're not going to fight Skeetch, right?" I ask.

Aaron laughs quietly. "Yeah, we're totally going to duel."

"I'm being serious, Aaron."

He puts both hands on my shoulders and looks me in the eyes.

"I'm going to go make sure Jess gets her stuff and that she finds a different place to sleep tonight. That's it. Those guys are probably all so stoned by now, they won't even notice me. Okay?"

I still don't move toward the van, and he sighs. Finally he reaches out his pinky finger and says, "I swear I'll be safe. That's the best I can do."

I nod, even though I don't want to. But even if I grabbed him and pulled him into the van, he'd just slip away later. So I raise my pinky and make him swear.

Before I get into the van he stops me and says, "Thanks, Abs."

BEFORE

THE HOUSE LOOKED SMALLER EMPTY. WITH ALL THE FURNITURE gone, I didn't recognize anything. The realtor had even painted over the pencil marks on the kitchen trim, Mom's faithful record of our growth. I stood there, pretending to look at the flyer that called our house "charming." Pretending not to be angry about all the people who were walking around, looking in every room as if nobody had ever lived here before.

I told Mom and Dad I was going for a run. We were going to be cooped up in the van for the next two weeks as we drove, and the motel they'd rented for those last few days wasn't much better. But I couldn't say I ended up back at the house by accident. From the outside, it looked the same as always. Gray siding with white shutters. A charcoal roof that slanted toward the front lawn. Even the wreath on the door—twisted vines Mom had taken off a tree long ago—was still in place. Nobody had wanted it, and what would we do with a wreath in California? The realtor called it character, but when I saw it sitting on the door it only depressed me.

The open house was scheduled for another hour, and I stayed the entire time. I went from room to room, smelling the drapes that still hung. Looking at the scarred wooden floors in Aaron's room. Everything about the house had our names written on it. How would any other family ever fit inside this space?

When it came time to leave, I couldn't do it. I asked the realtor for five minutes, and then ten after that. When we were thirty minutes past the original ending of the open house, she told me she needed to lock up. After she drove away, I went back to the porch and sat there until the sun began to set and the shadows reached across the front lawn in long fingers. When the van pulled up, I started to cry.

Mom came to the porch and sat next to me. I tried to dry my eyes, but the tears kept coming. Mom let me sit there like that for five minutes, not saying a word. When

I finally stopped crying, she put her arm around me and said, "I know. But we have each other, Abigail. And as long as we're together, nothing can beat us."

When I got in the van, Aaron was in the back. He wouldn't look at me. Even Dad was quiet. I told myself not to look at the house as we pulled away. That Mom was right. It was only a house, and we had a lot more than just that.

ELEVEN

MOM AND DAD ARE TRYING TO BE QUIET, BUT I HAVEN'T SLEPT all night. Aaron snuck back into the van just an hour before Dad got up and went outside to pee next to a tree hidden from traffic. At first, I was happy to hear their voices. I tried to let the soft monotone drag me to sleep. But then my fainting spell at Brother John's came back to me—was it only last night?—and now all I can do is lie here, pretending to be asleep, and wish they would go get breakfast without us.

If Aaron would wake up, he could be my distraction. Then I wouldn't have to talk to them about church. I wouldn't have to lie to them, or answer any questions. Because of course they're going to ask. Or maybe they'll take my hands and we'll pray for the sort of assurance that has been fueling Dad since we crossed the state line into California. Another easy answer to our problems.

When Dad finally goes for coffee, Mom sits silently until he gets back. Then they talk about the day, where we'll get breakfast and how Brother John may need them to help set up for tonight's service.

I should know better. They never go anywhere without us. When I open my eyes, Mom sees me first; she smiles and hands me something wrapped in a napkin. "Your father got these at the store. They were giving them away."

It's a croissant, probably days old now. I still eat it quickly. Dad sips from his coffee cup, looking as if he wants to say something. But only Mom talks.

"Did you sleep okay last night?"

"Pretty good," I say.

"You should take it easy today. Really get some rest."

As soon as she says it, Dad turns to her like he wants to object. Mom doesn't look at him, and he eventually goes back to his coffee. But taking it easy means sitting here, with them, and Dad won't be able to resist talking to me about God, or what I think my little episode means. Or worse: we'll end up in Brother John's office, looking to acknowledge the sign once again. Like I'm some kind of special pig and Dad's hoping for a prize.

I sit up and grab my shoes, still damp from last night.

"I'm going for a run," I say, forcing a quick smile. "I'll rest when I get back."

Under my quilt, I work my jeans up my legs. Dad flounders in the front seat, looking from me to Mom like his head is on a swivel. I stand up and make for the door without saying anything other than, "Thanks. Love you guys. Back later."

I take off as soon as I leave the van, letting the movement of my legs wipe away everything in my mind.

I run. Fast and hard until I'm doubled over at the entrance of the park—barely able to breathe. The trumpet man, only feet away from me, plays a few notes and then yells, "I am bound!" at a group of people trying to rent a bicycle. They pretend not to notice him.

Trumpet Man, however, wants their attention. He yells, "Wide extended plains!" and begins walking toward them, horn in hand. He's only a few steps away when the guy trying to rent bikes tells him to go away. Trumpet Man stops and again says, "Wide extended plains."

"I'm going to call the cops," the worker says, shooing

him away like a pigeon. Trumpet Man laughs loudly, his head back.

When he blasts a loud and long note, the bike manager comes from behind the desk swatting a stack of flyers in front of him. Trumpet Man jumps backward and then runs down the hill toward the tunnel. As the worker goes back behind the desk, he looks at me and says to the couple, "Sorry about that."

I stand up as he's talking, almost ready to start running again. As I cross the path, the woman renting the bike backs into me. Before I can apologize, the bike manager curses and says, "I'm so tired of all you homeless kids. Is it possible for me to rent bikes and not have you sit up here all day jerking off? Is that possible?"

"I'm not homeless," I say, shocked.

"Yeah, of course you're not," the man says. "Just get out of here, or I'll call the cops on you, too."

I turn around, careful not to mimic the trumpet man's movements—to draw any comparison between us. As I begin to run, I hear the man tell the people renting bikes, "You just have to be tough with them, that's all. Welcome to San Francisco!"

We aren't like the trumpet man, or even Jess and her

friends. One month doesn't change you, not in that way. There are people who go on the road for months, looking for adventure—trying to satisfy a primal wanderlust. Those are the ones we're like.

We can go back. We have a place.

I run through the tunnel, into the bright park, each footstep more of a denial than the last.

I push myself hard up and down the asphalt trails, blowing by moms with strollers and little kids yelling up to the sun. I run and run and run, but it doesn't make me feel better. It only makes my legs weak, enough that when I finally stop I have to lay in the grass. The coolness crawls up my back, prickling my skin at first. But as I lay there, my body relaxes and I can feel every blade of grass pushing against me.

If we are homeless now, at what point did it change? When we sold our house, technically. Even if we went back home, what happens next? There's no job for Dad. No warm bed waiting for any of us. We could sleep on Uncle Jake's couch, but that still isn't a home.

"Hey!" The voice startles me and I sit up fast. Jess stands there looking happy, but confused. She takes a long sip from a water bottle, as if she can't figure out what to say next. "Aaron's never around during the day. I think he might be a vampire."

"Okay . . ."

"I mean, I'm surprised to see you here. I'm happy, you know? Yay?"

She takes another sip from the water bottle and bites her lip before saying, "I can leave if you want. I realize I'm being kind of a freak."

"Join the club," I say, patting the grass. The truth is, any distraction would be welcome. Another freak added to the collection.

Jess sits next to me on the grass and offers me the bottle, which I take.

"So you're a runner? That's cool, I guess. Personally, I think running is for the birds. That's what my mom used to say about everything. Working, for the birds. Quitting smoking, for the birds. I'm officially adding running to that list."

I've almost downed the entire bottle as she says, "For. The. Birds."

Jess opens a granola bar and looks in the opposite direction, toward a group of people carefully turning their bodies, like slow-motion kung fu.

"That's definitely more my speed," Jess says. "Plus, ninja skills. So, bonus."

She chops the air and laughs.

"You run a lot?"

"I used to. In school."

"Oh. School." She breaks off half of her granola bar and hands it to me. "I would've given anything to get out of school a few years ago. For the birds, you know. Now, I think I'd like it."

"You could go back," I say.

Because if it could work for her, then maybe it would for us, too. You can start over, right? Even if it's something as small as going back to high school. There have to be do-overs, no matter how many times you need them.

She chews and swallows before saying, "Maybe. I don't know. What about you?"

"Oh, we go to Ford," I say, but it's rote. A programmed response that I'm not sure is still true. Do we still go to Ford? If we end up staying here, will we start a new school? I try to imagine wearing the same pants day after day. To have people figure out we live in our van. Is it something Mom and Dad have even considered?

"Maybe we'd be in the same class," Jess says. "How old are you?"

"Sixteen," I say.

"I'm seventeen," Jess says. "Eighteen if I'm trying to buy cigarettes."

She laughs, but doesn't say anything else until a thin man with at least three jackets on comes up and asks if she has a lighter. She hands one to him and says he can keep it.

"It's almost empty," she tells me. "So, whatever."

I've never smoked or even held a lighter except for the long ones they use to light the candles at church. The long silence is awkward, but I don't know if we have any common ground except age and Aaron. So that's where I start.

"Did Aaron come find you last night?"

She rolls her eyes and says, "Yeah, the idiot. I've been out here for a long time. I can take care of myself."

"He was worried, that's all."

She nods. "I know. But there are some things that you have to ignore. Some people, especially."

"Like Skeetch?" I ask.

I expect her to jump at his name. Instead, she bites the side of her thumbnail, inspecting it a few times before she sighs. "He is definitely candidate number one."

"How do you even know that guy?"

She laughs again, just as sad and sharp as the previous. "Can we not talk about it? I went over all of this with your brother last night and, honestly, right now, all I want to do is forget about Skeetch. Okay?"

I don't really want to think about him either, so I agree. Jess stands up and claps, so quickly I'm sure something's bit her. But then she pulls me up off the grass, too, and says, "All right, we need to get out of the park. See the world."

"Oh, I probably should get back to the van," I say. "I was only supposed to be gone for a quick run."

"Well, how long do you usually run?"

"An hour? Maybe?"

The truth is, sometimes back home I'd be gone for hours. Running through the cobblestone sidewalks of our downtown, waving at people from church. When I'd get back to the house, it would be dark and time for dinner. The food always tasted so good after those runs.

"An hour? That's plenty of time. Besides, I don't want to be alone."

I look up at the sky, as if there will be some kind of sign, an arrow in the clouds definitively saying, *Go back to the van; everything is fixed.* But the only clouds I see are a formless gray clump. And what do I have to go back to? Another five hours spent waiting in the van? Another conversation about God?

"All right, fine."

She leads me out of the park, past the bike seller who doesn't look up from his magazine, and up a hill until we're across the street from a train stop. People stand in one long jumbled line, all of them staring down the empty tracks.

"Are we taking the train?"

I must look crazy because she says, "Uh, yeah . . ."

It's not that I think she's going to lead me to some dangerous part of the city and leave me. But getting too far away from the van makes me nervous. I look up the street; the train still isn't visible.

"I don't have any money."

"Of course you don't, because you have a pass," Jess says. "Remember?"

I shake my head and she sighs. "Look, we're going to get on in the back of the train and act like we both have passes because, honestly, where we're going is really far and I'm not some runner chick. So let's try this again: you have a pass. Right?

"Oh," I say, "yeah."

She raises her eyebrows and nods, but I can't escape the nerves.

"Hey, nobody's dying here," Jess says. "We do it all the time. Cool?"

She smiles, hitting me gently on the shoulder. I smile back and say, "Yeah, cool."

"All right then. Let's do this."

She talks until the train comes. About Aaron, the city—every topic getting no more than a few seconds before she pivots and moves on. When the doors open, she talks all the way to the back of the car. I can feel every single person in the car looking at me, all of them waiting for me to produce this mythical pass. I wait for the conductor—do these trains have conductors?—to come charging toward us, ready to call the police.

I sit with my butt on the edge of the plastic seat, ready to jump up and run if I need to. But nobody says a word. If anything, it's as if we're not even on the train. Whenever I happen to make eye contact with somebody, they immediately look down or up—anywhere but at me. Even Jess eventually closes her eyes.

This is what it feels like to be invisible.

The speaker above us says, "Metro Civic Center Station/Downtown" and Jess pops up, shouldering her backpack in one quick movement. We follow the surge of people exiting the train out on to a street filled with cars and people. Jess doesn't stop the way I do, unsure of how to navigate these crowds. She turns left, and I have to run to catch up.

"If you ever come down here by yourself, you have to be careful," she says as we walk. "There's some really sketchy people around here sometimes."

We turn a corner, walking past a group of men working on the sidewalk. Without looking, Jess walks into the road, narrowly missing being hit by a car flying up the street. She ignores the horn, hoisting her middle finger into the air as she keeps walking. I wait for a delivery truck to squeeze down the narrow road before I follow. When I catch up to her she says, "And I never eat down here either. The big church down the road is always serving, but it's just too crazy in there. The line is stupid with assholes."

Mom and Dad have never brought us down here, and I can't say that I mind. It's hectic, dirty, and there seem to be men sitting against every building we pass, all of them whistling or slurring words through their thickly bearded faces. We walk two more blocks and right before turning another corner, Jess turns to me and says, "Okay, so I realize that the opportunity for disappointment exists. I think this is amazing. Not like Mount Rushmore amazing, mind you. But definitely better than, say, the mall. So make sure you gauge your expectation somewhere in between national treasure and mall."

I let my shoulders drop as I say, "Oh, I really hoped we were going to the mall."

She waits a moment, and then laughs, putting her arm around my shoulder. "Oh yeah, we're totally going to go get makeovers next. But first I need to get Dad's credit card. Hey, should we take your BMW or mine?"

I'm not sure what to expect when we go around the corner. But when I see the building, columns around it like a skeleton's ribs and a top that shines in the bright morning sun, I can't explain the excitement. It's only a building—city hall, I soon find out from a sign. But it's glorious and excessive and I love it.

We run the last block toward the building like kids unleashed in a theme park. From further away, I didn't notice the trees. But the closer I get, the more I'm captivated. They twist and knuckle up from the ground, hundreds of them flanking either side of an unnaturally green rectangle of grass. Their top branches are cut close to the trunk like bad haircuts. Jess bobs and weaves between them, her long red hair flying behind her.

I stop and stare at one of the trees—skinnier than the others, but unbelievably intricate. Thousands of lines connecting a map of bark.

"These are crazy," I say.

"Italian maples." She points to the cropped branches. "They cut the tops that way because they attract sutra beetles."

I stare at Jess, amazed. "How do you know that?"

She shrugs, turning away from me as if it's something anybody would know.

"I study botany in my spare time. No biggie."

This time, when she looks at me, a smile cracks her face. "Okay, I'm full of shit. I have no idea what these trees are called. But you believed it. These could totally be named Italian maples, right?"

I laugh, because if she hadn't smiled I would've gone back to the van and told Aaron the same thing. Like some kind of tree specialist. Jess and I walk through the trees, planted in straight lines that point to City Hall. I can't keep my hands off them. Each one feels different, new.

"Have you brought Aaron here?"

"No way. Boys are gross." And then almost immediately: "And especially now that I know he's got the hidden Idiot Gene. But at least he's good-looking, so that helps me overlook his moments of stupidity."

I can feel my face getting hot. Jess laughs.

"Oh God, I'm sorry. You probably don't want to hear about your brother's hotness. But hey, I promise I'll never tell you about the kissing. See what kind of friend I am?"

The first thing I think is: Are we friends? But then, almost immediately, I ask myself: Why not? It would be nice to have a friend. It would be nice to have somebody I could talk to who isn't connected by blood.

But I definitely don't want to hear about the kissing.

"Aaron isn't . . . hot," I say. "Is he?"

"Oh yeah. He definitely is," Jess says, smiling "But we're not talking about that because it's weird, right?"

"Yeah, pretty weird."

Jess leans against one of the trees and says, "Subject change. Did Aaron tell you how we met?"

"Oh yeah, right," I say. "He doesn't tell me anything."

"Idiot Gene. Again. We'll have to work on that.

Anyway, have you ever seen the guy who plays the trumpet in the park? He's really awful, so you'd remember him. I call him Stravinsky."

I don't mention that Stravinsky is violins, not trumpets. "Yeah, I know him."

"Okay, well I'd seen your brother in the park a few times, but mostly he just watched us from the trees—you know, we just thought he was another perv. That happens. You need to watch out for those freaks. Anyway, one day he comes running toward us like he was being chased by a bear or something."

Jess picks up an empty fast food bag and looks through it. "I guess Stravinsky was laying somewhere in the trees and your brother stepped on him and the psycho went nuts. Started chasing him, screaming the way he does. You've never heard anything like that. It was hilarious. We were all dying."

I try to imagine Aaron running away from the trumpet man and it brings a smile to my face. I wish I had been there to see it.

"Anyway, I'd found some money and went and got a Big Sip—have you seen those things? They're huge. I was drinking it when your brother came tearing up the hill and falls down, just atc it really hard in front of all of us. Normally, I'd laugh like crazy. But Stravinsky looked pissed and he was swinging that horn, so I stood up and threw my Big Sip right at him. I missed, but he got the message."

"Wow," I say.

"And that's how your brother became my personal slave," Jess says. "He's still earning off the seventy-nine cents I had invested in that soda."

She is lost in the memory and I don't want to ruin it, but this is the first conversation I've had in weeks that isn't about God, going home, or where the public showers can be found. We could be in the cafeteria at school, at the bus stop.

"When we were in middle school, I accidentally wrecked my mom's car."

Jess holds her hands out, shocked. "Hold up—what?"

"I broke my mp3 player and Aaron wouldn't let me borrow his," I say. "So I burned a CD and went out to the car."

"I was sitting on the driveway with the door open. Dancing." This part still embarrasses me, but Jess doesn't laugh. She looks completely enthralled. "And I wanted to listen to the song again, so I got in and tried to change it—but yeah, still dancing. I accidentally put the car in reverse. It rolled into the street and hit a tree. Ripped the driver's side door right off."

Jess fights the laughter at first, but soon she can't help it. "I'm sorry," she says. "That's horrible. Hilarious. But horrible."

I smile, too. "Well, Aaron came outside and was freaking out. Neither of us knew how to drive, but we decided it would be less of a shock if the car was back in the driveway. So Aaron got in and tried to put it back in the driveway. But he ended up driving right through the garage door."

"Stop it," Jess says. "Oh my God."

"And then of course my dad got home from work right then," I say. "Like, as Aaron was getting out of the car. It was smoking. There was wood and glass everywhere. Dad looked at Aaron, the car, and said, 'Well, you've had a good life, son.'"

Jess's laughing so hard she can't breathe. She holds her hands up for me to stop, but I'm on a roll.

"He tried to tell Dad it was my fault—that I crashed into a tree. And Dad wouldn't believe him. Because I'm the good one."

Jess is dying and I can't keep myself from laughing, either. We're holding each other up, cackling like idiots. The truth was, I felt bad about it for weeks. But every time I'd mention it, Aaron would get mad—wouldn't talk to me for hours, days. I don't know when it stopped stinging, or even the last time we laughed about it as a family.

But right now, it makes me feel closer to home—to him—than I have in a long time.

We take the train back to the same stop and walk slowly toward the park, still telling stories. How Jess once put deodorant on over her shirt because she didn't know any better. The time I wrecked my bike and Aaron passed out when he saw the gravel wedged under my knee. By the time we see Silas and E talking with Aaron, my stomach hurts from laughing. As soon as we come into view, Aaron strides toward us, E and Silas right behind him.

"What the hell, Abs? Where have you been?"

It doesn't seem like I left that long ago, but then I do the math.

"Are Mom and Dad mad?" I ask.

"How should I know? They went to the food bank two hours ago."

First I'm relieved, but then the shock hits. "Wait. They went without us?"

Aaron stares at me and says, "You act like you're disappointed."

I'm not sorry to miss standing in another line, waiting for another bag of random food. But I can't believe they left when I was still out running around the city, with Aaron sitting in the van alone. It's not like we're kids, but it still feels weird to be left behind.

"Were they mad before they went?"

At this, Aaron smiles. His entire body seems to relax. "Actually, yeah. Well, I guess they were more disappointed. As if that even matters now."

But it does matter to me. Even though there are times I'd kill to be more like Aaron, to not care what they think, it isn't as easy as simply cutting a string.

"Anyway, they told me to come find you. I'm sure we'll pray about it or something when they get back," he says. "But whatever. What were you guys doing?"

Jess pretends to lock her lips closed, tossing the imaginary key to me.

"Seriously?" Aaron asks. "You're not going to tell me where you went. Abs?"

I lock my lips, too. Aaron groans.

"We were doing girl stuff," Jess says. "Not anything an idiot boy who doesn't listen would enjoy."

"So, what? Having a pillow fight?" Silas says. "I saw that on cable once. Kinda hot."

"We were discussing botany," Jess says.

"The sutra beetle," I add.

When we start laughing, Silas looks confused.

Aaron drops his hands to his side and says, "Okay, fine. Whatever. We have to get back before Mom and Dad get sucked into the abyss without us."

"Yeah," E says. "Aaron was just telling us how your parents are primed and ready to disappear."

"Any day now," Aaron deadpans and I give him a look, because I don't want to talk about that with E or anybody else. I won't make fun of them, not like that. "What? Brother John promised. It's going to happen real soon."

"Oh shit. Brother John?" Silas says. "He actually calls himself Brother John?"

"It's like pastor," I say, but nobody's listening to me.

"Or as I like to call him," Aaron says, "the Body of Christ's Asshole."

E laughs until he sees me, stone-faced and staring at

Aaron. To his credit, he seems to be partially embarrassed.

"My bad," E says. "I didn't realize you liked him."

"What? No, Aaron's right. He is an . . . a-hole."

"A-hole?" Aaron laughs. "Seriously? How was the fifth grade last year, Abs? I hope your teacher wasn't a real butt face."

"It's not funny," I say, but it kind of is. And of course Aaron runs with it like it's an Olympic event.

"Sorry if I'm being a real d-word." He swipes his shaggy brown hair from his face—I don't know when he last got a haircut—and says, "A real s-head."

"You are being a real . . ." I try. I really do.

This gets all of them—Jess, Silas, and E, too. Silas says, "Mother-effer. You dang s-head!"

And even though they're laughing at me, I am miraculously not embarrassed. I laugh, too, the way I would at family dinners when Uncle Jake would give me a hard time about having a boyfriend. About any number of things. A happy discomfort.

"You can't do it!" Aaron says. "You can't! Oh, Abs."

Aaron cups his hands around his mouth and yells, "Shiiitttt! Fu-uh-ck!"

An older couple sitting on a bench and holding a

guidebook looks up. Another lady, pushing a stroller only steps away from us, shakes her head. Somewhere deeper in the park, a few teenagers yell something back, the words muddled by space, the trees.

When Aaron turns around he looks happy. Almost proud.

"They're just words, Abs. This isn't the Ten Commandments."

"I know," I say.

"How about a small one. *Piss? Shit.* Oh! *Ass.* That one's in the Bible. Remember, that one guy had a talking ass. It's approved."

"That was a donkey," I say.

"An ass is an ass," he says.

I could say it, but it always seemed unnecessary, a small thing I could do to be good. To be the type of person I wanted to be. But maybe he's right, maybe they are just words.

"Ass."

I wait. For a lightning bolt. A giant hand to come down from the sky. But all I can see is Aaron, putting his hand to his ear. All I hear are Jess and E, cheering. Telling me to say it again. So I do, a little louder. Aaron smiles.

"Praise the Lord! A true sister, let me hear you say *amen*!" He lifts his hands above his head, like he just won the game with a last-second shot. Running up and down the asphalt path, pretending to heal Jess and then E and Silas.

He puts his hands on their foreheads one at a time—"Be healed, brothers! Be healed, Sister!"—before pushing them to the grass, where they twitch and laugh. When Aaron finally circles back to me, I'm certain everybody in the park is now watching us.

"Sister, I need to hear a good word from you," he yells. It's uncanny how much he sounds like Brother John. "I said a good word, Sister! Amen! Praise that Lord! Uh-huh!"

Fine. If it doesn't matter. If nobody is watching or listening. Fine.

"Oh, Brother Aaron! I just need some healin'!"

My falsetto, the way I put my hand to my forehead, almost break Aaron out of character. He smiles, raises his hands to the sky—speaking to the bugs in the trees, to the trumpet man, who's close now, curious.

"Sister, do you feel the Lord?"

I laugh and say, "Oh yeah. Totally."

Trumpet Man nods, too, and says, "Wide extended plains! I am bound!"

"Okay, man. That's cool," Aaron says, gently pulling away as Trumpet Man reaches for him. The game seems to be over, and I'm surprised to be disappointed. Not to be able to fall and shriek and convulse the way Jess, E, and Silas still are. But the way Aaron looks at me, as if I've finally unlocked whatever's tied him together over the past few weeks, is enough.

"We should probably get out of here," I say. "That guy makes me nervous."

Aaron shakes his head, his eyes focused right on mine.

"I told you: I need a good word, Sister." His voice is low, loud enough only for me. My mind reels through all the Bible verse I know. Those words. But Aaron sees right through me. He shakes his head again and says, "I said a good word."

He doesn't have to push me this time. It slips off my tongue, so easy.

"Shit," I say.

Aaron throws his hands in the air once again.

"She's been healed! You hear that, brothers and sisters! Healed!"

And then he pushes me into the grass, right next to Jess and the boys. All of us laugh as Trumpet Man chases

Aaron across the grass. Aaron stops, moves—not letting the man ever get too close. When he finally gives up, sitting down with the trumpet in his lap only a few feet away from us, Aaron is bent over gasping, smiling bigger than I thought was still possible.

TWELVE

I SIT NEXT TO AARON ON THE HILL. JESS HAS HER HEAD IN HIS LAP, nearly asleep.

"You feel better," he says. "Admit it."

I look past him, toward the sky. The sun shines bright, burning little spots in my vision, but I don't stop watching, waiting—I'm not sure if I'm happy or devastated that nothing happened when I said those words. Maybe we can all do whatever we want and nobody really cares either way.

"A little," I say. "Yes."

Aaron shakes his head. "Hell yes."

I smile, but it's mannequin-like. We've learned how to fake our way through everything. And even when the happiness is real, it's followed by an almost instant panic. As if my body knows it can't last.

"Oh, c'mon Abs. This is supposed to be fun."

"I'm fine," I say.

But if I'm being honest, I'm not. I don't want to say this to Aaron because he still seems so happy, but everything I've ever known is disappearing and I can't stop it.

What did it feel like before Brother John? I try to go backward and replay everything that's happened. And for the first time, I wonder if I'm the one who's really changed.

I hear Skeetch before I see him. He's laughing loudly, coming from behind a tree with his arms around two girls. When Aaron sees him, he moves Jess's head from his lap and tells me, "Stay with Jess."

Aaron walks straight up to Skeetch—he's going to punch him. Something. I reach over to nudge Jess, but she's already standing up and walking toward them. I follow her, surprised when Skeetch tries to slap Aaron's hand. Like they're old buddies.

"What are you doing?" I ask Aaron.

He doesn't answer. Jess grabs him by the arm and says, "He's being an idiot. That's what he's doing."

"Jess, c'mon," Aaron says.

"Don't *c'mon* me. We talked about this."

Aaron tries to touch her shoulder and she steps back. Skeetch laughs and says, "This is why we never worked out, Jess. You're up in everybody's business. Oh, and you're a total pain in the ass."

"Back off," Aaron says.

"Hey man, I'm with you. Team Aaron."

Aaron ignores him and turns to Jess. "Why don't we go talk somewhere?"

"No," she says.

The rest of the group begins copying her—No! No! No!—followed by laughter. Aaron looks embarrassed, but Jess is fierce. When Aaron tries to touch her again, she grabs her backpack and walks over to me.

"I hope you guys have a nice life, because I'm done with this shit."

And then she's gone. Aaron doesn't move, even though I can tell he wants to chase her down. Skeetch watches her, too. He slaps Aaron on the shoulder and says, "Young love. What a bitch."

Aaron ignores him, still watching Jess. When she's just a smudge of a person walking toward the entrance of the park, Aaron turns to me and says, "I'm taking you back to the van."

"Whoa, hold up a second," Skeetch says. "We've got business. Remember? You coming to me and being all *I need to make some money, can you help me, Skeetchy?*"

"Later," Aaron says.

"Later?" Skeetch says. "I don't know what you think this is, but your ass needs to go stand at the entrance of the park. Right now."

Aaron swallows down whatever he wants to say and turns back to me. "Go to the van. I'll be back soon."

"What's going on?" I ask.

"I'm getting us out of here," he says. "That's all you need to know."

"What does that mean?"

"Look at you being all coy and shit," Skeetch says. "Tell Little Sis what's up. Tell her how Skeetch is hooking you up. Some viable employment skills happening here."

"Listen, asshole," Aaron starts. But his words are drowned out by Skeetch's laughter.

"Asshole? You ask me for help and then call me an asshole? Okay. I get it. But, how should I put this? Oh yeah, fuck you. You don't need my help, fine. I don't give a damn.

Any of these kids will sell shit. Any single one of them."

Neither Skeetch nor Aaron move until Skeetch puts a hand in Aaron's face and says, "You know what? Find your own way back to Alabama or wherever your hick ass is from. I'm done with this bullshit."

When Skeetch walks away, Aaron drops his head and doesn't move. Behind him, E pretends to look for something in his backpack as Silas studies his hands.

"Let's go," he says.

"Are you kidding me? What was that about?" I ask.

"Can we not do this here?" he says. "Please?"

Aaron follows me out of the park. I take the same path as Jess, past Trumpet Man, who yells out, "Happy place!" When we reach the entrance, Aaron stops and looks down the street. Jess is gone.

"Before you say anything," Aaron says, "it's not a big deal."

"Oh, that must be why Jess freaked out. I mean, it's all pretty normal besides the part where you and Skeetch are friends."

"We're not friends. He's a dick."

"Oh, great," I say. "That clears everything up. And by the way, I'm not a complete idiot. I can guess what's going on."

He walks fast up the street, and I have to nearly run to keep up with him. When I tell him to slow down, he picks up the pace. I stop in front of an older apartment building with a "For Sale" sign in the window.

"Please talk to me."

Aaron turns and kicks the gate of a doorway. It rattles loudly, the sound hammering against the enclosed porch. He grabs it with both hands and puts his forehead against the frame. He mumbles something I barely hear, and when I ask him what he said, he turns around and looks at me.

"I said . . . I've got it under control."

He reaches out and takes my hand, squeezing it once. His face dull and vacant.

"I'm getting us out of here. Okay?"

"Aaron . . ."

"Please, Abs."

A family passes us, the man carrying a small girl on his shoulders. Aaron watches them for a second before starting to walk. The girl chatters on as her father lifts her above his head and then carefully down to the street. When they stop in front of a large house, we catch up with them. The little girl looks at us and says, "Hello!"

Aaron doesn't say anything back, but I smile. I don't make eye contact with her parents, because I don't want to see their fear or disgust, whatever they think of us. Aaron walks with his head down against the wind, which has picked up, and I try to stay warm behind him.

We turn left, onto the street where the van is, and my stomach tightens slightly. On top of everything else, we've also been gone way too long. I'm trying to figure out how I'll respond to the I Can't Believe You'd Do This speech—how I'll convince Aaron that he doesn't need to do anything for Skeetch and we don't need to leave—when Aaron stops. I almost run into him.

"The van was right here," he says.

I look up the street. It feels familiar, but that doesn't mean a thing. We've parked on this block at least ten times now.

"Are you sure?" I ask, pointing up the street. "It could be on the next block."

"It was right here," he says, pointing to a small natural food grocery store across from us. "Before I came to the park, I went in there and got a cup of water. It was right here, in this spot."

We both stare at the small red car that sits there now.

"Maybe they needed it at the food bank," I say. But that never happens. Ever. I peer further down the street, as if straining my eyes will make Mom and Dad appear.

Mom always used to worry about us getting lost in the grocery store, at the mall—whenever we'd go to the county fair. Before we'd walk into those places, she'd pull us aside and remind us to stay in one place if we got separated. That as soon as she saw us gone, nothing would keep her from finding us. Be still and wait. That has always been the plan.

I turn to Aaron. "They probably had to move the van so we didn't get a ticket. I'm sure it's somewhere on this street."

He nods, but his agreement doesn't make me feel better as we begin walking. Because it still means they left us to figure that out for ourselves. I listen for Dad's laugh, Mom's voice, hoping it will rise above everything like a dream—calling us to them.

We search every corner of the street, but the van isn't here.

I almost take Aaron's hand again, because the farther we go, the more the panic grows inside me. Even Aaron looks worried, and as much as I've wanted him to feel something for Mom and Dad—anything—seeing him this way only makes it worse.

"Did they tell you to meet them at Brother John's?" I ask, hoping he forgot. That he would brighten up and say, *Oh yeah!*

He shakes his head.

"We should check," I say. "It's only a few blocks away."

I don't know what else to consider. If they are at the church—how is that any better?

I'm not sure if Aaron or I take the first step, but it doesn't really matter. As we walk, I put every emotion—every ounce of belief—into one final message, shot straight to the sky.

Please let there be a good reason.

It doesn't take long, and soon we're staring at the same cars that are always in the parking lot. I don't see the van and I panic. If they're not here, I have no idea where else to look. I have no idea what we'll do tonight, tomorrow. The city is huge, big enough that you could get lost forever. You could lose somebody without any trouble.

"Maybe Dad left Mom here," Aaron says. But before he opens the door, he pauses. Like he's making his own deals with God.

When we walk inside, Brother John stands in the center of the room, surrounded by ten people spread across the floor like corpses. They're all praying—different words, different voices—but it seems uniform. One machine with a multitude of parts, working with exact precision.

The noise of the door clicking closed behind us is small, but the sound is like a shotgun going off in the small room. Brother John lifts his eyes, lasers pointed at Aaron and me. Slowly, heads lift from the floor. Then I hear Mom's voice.

"Aaron? Abigail?" At her voice, our names, Dad stands up—the first to separate from the group. When he reaches us, he looks worried. Mom comes right behind him.

"Are you okay?"

Aaron's face goes wooden. His lips, glued together.

"We couldn't find the van," I say, almost whispering.

"What do you mean you couldn't find the van?" Mom asks.

I turn to Aaron, but all he's doing is staring at Dad.

"Dale."

Brother John says nothing else. But it's enough to make Dad formal, completely foreign. He straightens up and puts on this counterfeit smile.

"We're almost finished, kids," he says. "Why don't you wait outside?"

Dad never calls us *kids*. He never dismisses us so easily. I almost think it's a joke, but then he turns around and lies back down on the floor with the rest of the people. I stare at Mom, but all she does is squeeze my hand once and says, "It's okay, it's okay. We'll figure this out."

Outside, Aaron kicks at a cigarette butt. It barely moves. How did it even get into the parking lot? Nobody here smokes. And there aren't any visitors. Aaron continues scuffing at it, doing anything to avoid what we both want to say. Every few seconds, he looks at the door and frowns even deeper.

I am not surprised this is where we found them, but I cannot square it in my mind. When would've they realized it had been hours since they'd seen us? That the city had gone dark and—oh no!—their children are sitting on the sidewalk. Of course, they wouldn't know about the van. Because they were here. Like always.

We're supposed to be the irresponsible ones—not them. We're supposed to be the ones who make bad decisions and stare at the floor while they explain how our choices will affect our future. How will they be able to tell us to do anything ever again?

"They have no idea where the van is," I say. Even as the words come out of my mouth, I can't believe it. "It probably got towed."

"It doesn't matter. We're leaving, Abs. I don't care if we have enough money. We're going. Tonight."

The world stops as he says it, only to speed up again and throw everything off-balance.

"I don't want to go," I say. I can feel the tears behind my eyes, threatening.

"Well, get over it. Because I'm not leaving you with them."

"No, you get over it," I say. "Unlike you, I haven't been waiting to ditch Mom and Dad since we got here."

His eyes grow bigger. His mouth trembles with whatever he's about to say next.

"They ditched us!" he yells, his voice growing higher and higher until it breaks. "They are never going to leave this bullshit. Never. So this is it. Go time. Right now."

He reaches for my hand and when I step away, Aaron looks like I've broken him in half.

"They don't give a damn about us, Abs. Not anymore."

Behind him, the door opens. It's like a movie, the way the light pours out into the parking lot—the way Brother John is backlit, as if he's arriving straight from heaven. Aaron turns on him.

"What? Are we inconveniencing you? Are we making it difficult for you to hear God's plan?" Brother John watches him without a word, which infuriates Aaron even more. "You know this is all bullshit, right? You have to know it. The world is ending! Sell all your shit! Did anyone really believe that?"

Brother John doesn't flinch. Doesn't take his eyes off Aaron, who steps forward like he wants to throw a punch.

"Oh yeah, I forgot—they believed that." Brother John turns and looks at Mom and Dad, standing in the doorway next to him.

"Tell me I'm wrong," Aaron says. "I dare you."

But Brother John doesn't. He turns around and walks back into the church, stopping only to say something to Dad, who looks more horrified than concerned. He nods and walks to Aaron.

"No," Aaron says, all the fight gone. His eyes won't leave Brother John's back as he disappears into the church. "Come back out here!"

"Son—" Dad tries to touch his shoulder, but Aaron jumps back.

"This is your fault," he says, slowly backing away.

Aaron stares at Dad. From behind me, a hand comes to my shoulder—Mom. Dad takes a step forward, his hands out. Aaron takes another step back.

"I understand," Dad says. "Nobody's mad at you."

Dad gets a few steps on him, an arms-length away. Before Aaron realizes what's happening, Dad has him wrapped up tight. I want to believe he'll apologize, promise that we'll all go back to normal. But I hear his words ringing across the parking lot, every one of them nothing more than fiction.

"This is the right thing," he says. "We're all going to be fine. This is where we're supposed to be. Just come inside and—"

When Dad falls to the ground, I don't realize Aaron pushed him until I see his face. It's fear, panic, and, worst of all, resolve. Dad pulls himself up to one elbow, then to a knee. And in the time it takes for him to get to his feet, Aaron looks away from him—right at me.

I need to do something—and I don't know what, but something; I should do something. Aaron turns and sprints away, dodging a car and then a bus, disappearing into the busy streets. Mom grabs my arm. Dad's mouth opens and he runs to the road. A line of cars stop him. But it doesn't matter: Aaron is gone.

Everything rushes back.

The air into my lungs, the dizzy reality of what happened, and the sound. Cars passing on the street, the murmur of people inside the church. And me, screaming Aaron's name; hoping it cuts through the city and makes him stop.

THIRTEEN

DAD MAKES ME GO INSIDE THE CHURCH WITH HIM AND MOM. Brother John is already in his office, the radio receiver flipped on. It hums as he tests the microphone. People stand at the side of the room, watching us. Me.

"We need to find Aaron," I say. "And I think the van got towed."

Mom looks into Brother John's office and then at Dad. "Go tell him."

"That was a tithe," Dad says. "A gift for God, Kat."

"I don't care," Mom says. "Do you hear me? I don't care. If you don't, I will. I swear I'll go right in there and tell him exactly what he can do with all of this."

"What are you talking about?" I ask.

They both turn to me. Mom tries to smile as she says, "Don't worry about it, honey. It's okay. We're okay."

But we're not okay. We're so far from okay that I can't believe she even said it. Every time something happens, that word comes out. And that's when I realize what they're talking about.

"No," I say.

Dad's eyes shift around the room, like a fly. Landing on the floor, the wall, the door—but never me. Mom tries to hug me, but I won't let her. I can't believe it.

"You gave him the money from that church? All of it?"

"He needed it, Gabs," Dad says. "People need to know it's still happening."

"Your father is going to get it back," Mom says. "And then we're going to find your brother."

Dad moves toward Brother John's office in a sheepish stutter-step, a far cry from his old hell-raising days—that's how Uncle Jake always talked about Dad. As soon as it would pass from Jake's lips, Dad would demur. Go to another room, like that would keep me and Aaron from hearing about the days when he'd drink cheap wine in the North Carolina hills, running bare chested through the woods. Dad like we've never seen him. Maybe like he wished never existed. Is he worried about how he looks now? What I think now?

I follow Dad into Brother John's office. Mom tries to stop me, but I dodge her and go stand next to Dad, waiting for him to open his mouth. Brother John turns away from his receiver, considering us for a second before he says, "Do you need me, Brother Dale?"

Dad hems and haws for a second before finally saying, "It's about the money, Brother John. We need some of it back. Our van got towed and I need to go find my son."

"Well, Brother Dale," he says, "that money's already been committed to God's will."

Dad nods. I try to stare at Brother John with the same thinly veiled contempt Aaron conjures. For the first time it comes easily.

"Well, without the van," Dad says. "We don't have a place to stay."

"You can sleep right here, in the house of God," he says. "Is there anything better than that?"

Dad doesn't answer, but he doesn't move, either. Brother John looks confused. "Brother Dale, you know God has everything planned, right? God isn't in the business of taking away things we need."

I can't stop myself. I practically scream.

"Are you serious?"

"Abigail," Dad says.

"It's okay, Brother Dale," Brother John says, holding up his hands. "There is a time for questions. But, Sister Abigail, there is also a time to stop asking questions. You need to trust that this is the place for you to be. You need to trust that God is working right now. With God, what is up can be down. What is right can seem wrong. You need to trust and believe that God works in fearful and mysterious ways."

He thinks for a second, then adds, "I wouldn't be surprised if losing your brother and that van isn't God working right now. Trying to teach you an important lesson. I say we pray for some discernment, Brother Dale."

Something comes loose inside me. Maybe it's a pin falling out, the last thing holding together my composure or my ability to pretend—something. Whatever it is, I speak to Brother John—really—for the first time.

"Pray? You want to pray about this?"

"God is telling your family something," Brother John says.

"God didn't do this. . . ."

He cocks his head to the side, like he didn't understand me. Then he nods carefully and says, "You only assume He didn't. Sometimes God removes things from our lives for our own benefit. Distractions. Things that pull us away from Him. And Brother Dale, I'm sorry, but your son has been a distraction ever since you arrived. Sometimes we must give up much to gain the Kingdom of God."

We've got to give up more. Us. The ones who've spent how many weeks sleeping in our van and barely eating? When was the last time Brother John gave up anything? I turn to Dad, grabbing his hand.

"Dad, please. Aaron isn't a thing. And we don't need to pray about this. We need to go."

Because forget the van. We can take a bus home. Forget the fact that we have no place to sleep tonight. We can stay in one of the shelters. Or I can find a job and so can he. We can do whatever it takes to fix this, to start over. All we need to do is move.

I search Dad's face for even the smallest flicker, but it's blank. He says, "Gabs, I think I should talk to Brother John alone for a few minutes."

When I turn back to Brother John, I swear I'm going to knock that huckster smile off his face.

But the lamp is closer and I grab it right off his desk—throwing it across the room. Seeing it smash against the wall makes something inside me jump, a nervous happiness that I want to feel again and again until there's nothing left of this office. Hearing Brother John yell only deepens the pleasure. Dad tries to stop me, but I lunge for the desk, scattering papers and throwing books. I kick over the cheap folding chair and then pick it up and throw it across the room, too. When I move to the radio equipment, Dad pins my arms against my body and pulls me into a bear hug.

"Abigail, enough!"

Mom runs into the office, her mouth in a horrified circle. But I don't care about appearances or what anybody in this damn church thinks. It doesn't matter. If they're not going to help me find Aaron, I'll do it myself. And then we'll leave. Me, him, Jess. We'll go back to North Carolina and never think about any of this ever again.

"Put her down, Dale," Mom says. And he does. But carefully, like I still might make a run at the radio equipment.

Brother John smooths the wrinkles on the front of his pants, sighing as he walks around the desk. He looks at me for a long time, but I refuse to look away from him.

Refuse to give him the satisfaction of my obedience. Not anymore.

"This is all a joke," I say.

I've spent my whole life believing God was working in the world. That I was somehow good because of that belief. Pastor Jamie always said that doubt wasn't enough to keep you away. That God would always be tapping on your shoulder or jumping out in front of you. Always giving you a chance.

But I don't care what chances God or Brother John are giving. Not anymore. Whatever wires got crossed, whichever part is broken inside me, I don't care. I'll leave it unplugged for the rest of my life if it means having to be a part of this world. I can survive without Brother John or God. And if I have to, without Mom and Dad.

Dad turns to me and says, "Abigail, you need to apologize to Brother John."

Of course I'm the one who needs to apologize, because that's the most important thing. God forbid we get on the wrong side of Brother John! Here's a novel idea: how about Brother John apologizes to me? Because unless I'm going to take everything away from him, that's not happening. Not even close.

I turn around and walk out of the office without a word, heading straight for the door.

Dad races after me, blocking my escape. He doesn't say anything and Mom is just as quiet. The church is empty now, the initial spectacle having worn off. Dad watches me, but I won't look at him. I won't be the first one to say anything.

"You denied God," he says, almost to himself. "You can take it back—God will let you take it back, Gabs."

I could claim crossed fingers—that I didn't really mean it. As if using certain words will make me snap back together, back into the good girl I've always been. The one they are comfortable having sit in the backseat of the van doing—what? Nothing. I haven't done a single thing to help us since we've been here. But that's changing. Right now.

"I didn't deny God. I denied him."

Dad looks to Brother John's office, afraid he heard me.

"Dad, Aaron's gone," I say.

"I know," he says.

"Then why are we here!"

I try to push past Dad, but he holds me in place, searching my face.

"I can't make your brother come back," he says. "All I can do is hope and pray that God keeps him safe."

The words hollow me.

"That's all you can do? He's gone, Dad. We need to go find him because nobody else is going to do it. Not Brother John. Not God. That's the only thing we should be worried about right now."

What I'm saying scares him; I can see it in his eyes, the way his shoulders tense and his grip tightens. But scared of what? Who?

Dad composes himself and lets go of me.

"You don't have to trust me, Abigail. But now is a time when it would be good to trust God."

He looks up, a last-chance hope slathered embarrassingly across his face. As if I'm going to wrap my arms around him and say, *Yes! God is going to fix everything!*

"I can't," I say. "Not if you're staying here."

I could keep going, could list all the other reasons why I don't trust anything other than what I can do for myself—not anymore. But what would it matter? He isn't listening. He's waiting. For me to say the words that will make him feel better. For some joke. And that only leaves one choice, a decision I made as soon as he chose Brother John over Aaron.

I will hurt him.

I will leave.

But I don't know if even that will work.

I don't say a word when Mom asks if we're going to go look for Aaron. Dad shakes his head and mumbles something about consistency and how Aaron knows where we are. That he'll come back when all his steam is gone.

Aaron was right. Mom and Dad will never see that they made a mistake. They'll never turn away from Brother John. I only hope that he hasn't left already. That he and Jess aren't on some bus right now, headed anywhere but here.

Dad stands guard at the door until the sun begins to drop and the small room grows dark. I force patience into my body, reminding myself that he'll be asleep soon enough. And when that happens, I'm gone.

If anything, I'm really good at waiting now.

I lay there, refusing to use the couch cushions Brother John produces from his office, or to get warm under the threadbare blanket he hands Dad before leaving. Mom is right next to me, huddled under her and Dad's jackets. She isn't using the blanket, either. Across the room, Dad sits against the door with his head raised. I can barely hear him, but even the soft words of his prayers sound like cannon blasts in my ears.

When Dad finishes praying, he comes close to my face and whispers my name. I pretend not to hear him, to be asleep—Aaron's best trick. He stands there for a moment before quietly putting the blanket over my body. In the faint light, through half-closed eyes, I watch as he lies next to Mom, wrapping his long arms around her body.

Outside, a couple of teenagers laugh and yell, but we're all used to this now—the constant movement, the sounds—and when a bottle breaks, nobody reacts. The teenagers move down the block, and then it's quiet again.

I wait for an hour before I stand up. I move deliberately in the direction of the bathroom, in case Mom and Dad aren't fully asleep. I walk around the room—I could be going to pray—and eventually circle back to our makeshift bed. Mom and Dad haven't even stirred.

The first thing I do is go to Brother John's office, which isn't locked. I grab anything that might be useful. A small backpack, a flashlight with extra batteries. In his desk drawer I find ten dollars, but before I take it I pause.

I have never stolen anything in my life.

I try not to think about God, about what I said—who I've become. But again, nothing has happened. No lightning bolts. No boils or clouds of insects. And while the emptiness—that sense of loss—is still there, I do my best to ignore it. To give God a taste of what it feels like.

I take the ten dollars and walk out of his office.

The light from the liquor store washes over Mom and Dad in electric red. I hurry to the door and don't look back.

FOURTEEN

THE NIGHT IS COLD, MORE SO THAN IT HAS BEEN. I RUN TO keep warm. And if I'm being honest, to keep myself from completely breaking down. Because that's what I want to do—cry until I empty myself of every emotion, even the ones I don't want to lose. When I get to the entrance of the park, Trumpet Man is sitting there holding his trumpet. He stares at me, surprised.

But whatever interest he has initially vanishes, and he goes back to working the valves on his instrument. I stand there, shivering, and try to think. I'm almost certain Aaron's in the park. But where? It's huge and, at night, covered in shadows seemingly designed to hide the people who sleep there. Indistinct voices rise up from within the walls as Trumpet Man raises his horn and plays one soft note.

"No chilling winds," he says. "No poisonous breath."

I jog down the path, hoping I'll find Aaron and Jess with the rest of the group, talking on the hill. But they're not. A few people I don't know are asleep on the grass, hidden under thick blankets. I run further into the park, stopping whenever I hear a voice or a cough in the darkness.

I've run for almost ten minutes when I see the wave, carrying a girl high above the rest of the park. Tall and spindly, she walks cautiously across the cresting water, and then disappears suddenly, like she was pulled under.

And then there she is again, walking on top of the wave, arms stretched out like wings.

But it's not a girl and the water is just a sculpture, blue and white concrete that forever breaks away from the park and toward the playground. It's Skeetch. He places one foot in front of the other, like a gymnast on a high beam. When he looks down at me, he says, "Look at me. Just like Jesus!"

He jumps off the sculpture and jogs over to me. Someone appears to the left of us, bundled for the cold, but shuffles into the darkness, disappearing. My instinct is to run, but I have no idea where else Aaron could be so I stand there, trying to seem relaxed.

"Where's Aaron?"

"You know, that's a damn good question. Where is that brother of yours? I've been looking for him all night."

When he takes another step toward me, I put up my fist and he laughs. "Seriously? What is it with you and that bitch ass brother of yours? Always starting trouble when people are trying to help."

He reaches forward and moves a piece of hair away from my face, letting his finger linger on my temple.

My hand is a blur. It meets Skeetch's nose, but doesn't do much. He pushes me against the sculpture hard, bruising my back and holding my hands above my head. There's onion on his breath and he hasn't showered in who knows how long. When he reaches to wipe the hair out of his eyes, I try to move. He pushes me hard against the cement sculpture and laughs.

"I'm not going to hurt you," he says, leaning close to whisper in my ear. "Unless that's what you want."

He smiles, letting go of my hands long enough for me to reach out and claw him. His skin rips under my nails. I feel the blood. In pure instinct, I put my knee between his legs as hard as I can, again and again until he falls on the ground.

"You fucking bitch," he groans, reaching for my leg—anything. But I'm already running.

I don't know where I'm going, but I move as fast as I can. I keep imagining Skeetch behind me, coming from the shadows, grabbing me. My stomach cramps like I'm sick, like I'm going to throw up, but I don't stop. When I see the lights from a road ahead of me, I run straight through a small thicket of trees, dodging the trunks and branches until I'm under the yellow streetlights.

A car honks when I cut in front of it. The driver yells. I take turns blindly, working myself deeper into the city, as far away from the park as I can get. As I careen around a corner, I trip, crashing to the sidewalk in a heap.

The pavement is cold and sticky and I can't breathe. I'm sucking in air wildly, but I can't make my chest expand—can't bring in any air. I can feel Skeetch's hands on my body, can smell his breath. Everything that's happened falls on top of me, every brick of emotion that I've kept stacked crumbles one after the other, and when I finally do breathe, it's in one long cry.

I try to stand up, but my legs quiver with exhaustion.

Every breath feels like needles being stuck deep into my lungs.

Across the street, a voice asks if I'm okay. It's a couple, maybe college aged. When they come closer, the man leans down and reaches out to touch my forehead, which I only now realize stings. I flinch and try to scoot away from him on my hands.

"Whoa, hey—it's okay."

"I'm sorry," I say. "I'm fine."

The woman whispers into the man's ear and he nods. She pulls out her cell phone and says, "We're going to call an ambulance."

I shake my head and stand up, forcing my legs to hold my weight. My entire body burns under my clothes. I start to walk away and the man says, "Hey—really. Stay still."

I move down the sidewalk. I can't waste time with an ambulance, the questions that will inevitably come at the hospital. Where are your parents? Where do you live? Nothing I can answer, at least easily. Not anymore. So I walk away as fast and normally as I can, trying to catch my breath every few seconds. Trying to get off the street. Hoping Aaron will magically appear.

I hurry around a corner and wait inside the doorway of a closed storefront, listening for footsteps—any evidence that Skeetch is coming. For an ambulance's siren. The small space blocks the wind, but it's still cold—too cold to stand still without a blanket or a decent jacket. Everything I have is locked up in the van.

When my toes begin to lose feeling, I step out of the doorway and move as quickly as I can.

I walk for an hour, trying to ignore the cold as it climbs from my toes to my legs and eventually across my entire body. By the time I see the large church—where we sometimes eat dinner, where they gave us the money—I can't stop my body from convulsing with the cold.

The door we use to line up for food is locked, as is every other door and window. But a huge black gate around the side of the building swings in the wind so I go through and close it behind me, if only to escape the wind for a little bit. The alley is filled with signs, old tables, and a collection of hoses. The two church buildings rise above me like twin giants, casting a shadow so deep that I can barely see anything except a subtle light at the end of the alley.

I step carefully down the alley until I reach a small window at the base of one of the buildings. The heating system churns and gurgles behind the small pane of glass. I reach down and push on it. At first, the window doesn't move, just dust and dirt spiraling into the air. But when I push harder, it rotates inward so the heat pours out onto my hands, my neck, my face. Heaven.

When my hands and face are warm, I stick my feet through the small opening. As the heat warms my toes, I study the window—it's no smaller than the dog door at home. How many times did Mom forget her keys and accidentally lock us out of the house, only for me to wiggle through that small rectangle and let us back in?

I manipulate the rest of my body through the small window, lowering myself onto the concrete floor of the room. Once inside, my heart starts beating fast. What if there's an alarm? Can I get out of this little room, which, now that I'm in it, is boiling? I try the only door in the room and it opens easily. I brace myself for the screech of an alarm, but the only thing I hear are the gasps and groans of the heater working behind me.

An exit sign gives off enough light for me to see the room, large and carpeted. I walk across it slowly, expecting the lights to pop on at any second. But nothing happens. I move slowly through the dark church, opening doors and looking in the rooms, jumping every time the heating system kicks on.

It's creepy, but warm. Enough that when I see a couch in one room, I almost lie down. I'm so tired I can barely keep my eyes open, and the idea of sleep sounds wonderful. But I can't fall asleep here. I can't risk someone recognizing me from eating here with Mom and Dad, or calling the police.

When I find the sanctuary, the Christmas trees are still lit. I stare at them from the hallway, the lights swimming together as my eyes lose focus. How much time have we lost in rooms just like this one? Sitting around and waiting for something to happen to us. None of us ever doing anything. Somebody has to act. And if God wants in on this, fine. He can jump in. But I'm done waiting.

I wander around the building, trying to amuse myself with anything I can find to keep me awake until sunlight begins sneaking through the windows. Magazines on an end table. A pocket-sized pinball machine in what looks like the teen room. I treat myself to two packages of cookies in the kitchen. When I find a room filled with toddler toys, I almost turn to leave. Then I see the phone. A phone.

I push the familiar pattern of numbers, burned into

my memory from a childhood of calling with errands and begging to go fishing whenever Mom and Dad weren't around. Uncle Jake is the sort who always answers his phone on the first ring, maybe the second. Like he knew when we needed something. But I'm still not sure he'll answer until I hear his voice.

"Hello?"

I slide down the wall, holding the phone against my ear. I can barely choke out a response, anything.

"Abigail? Is that you?"

"Yes," I say, and there's silence on the other line. A long enough silence that I'm not sure if this was a good idea. Maybe we've been gone longer than I thought, somehow fell asleep, forgotten like Rip Van Winkle.

"Good God, Abigail . . . ," he finally says. "Are you okay?"

"I'm sorry," I say. What time is it in North Carolina? Here? I look out the window at the sky, suddenly unsure if he's working nights at the mill. "Did I wake you up?"

"Wake me up? You know better than to ask me a question like that," Uncle Jake says. "You call me anytime and I'm answering that phone, okay?"

Hearing his voice and how we fall back into this natural

rhythm like nothing has changed tightens something in my throat. Like I'm still 5.2 miles away from his house and asking him to come pick me up.

"You still there?"

"I'm here," I say, swallowing again and again, trying to push down the fears and, maybe, the pride.

"Could you come get us?"

The line is silent for a second. Then: "Yeah. Of course."

"Or send me and Aaron some money. That would work, too." It comes out so fast that it probably surprises Uncle Jake as much as it did me. "I'm sorry to ask for it so bluntly, but Aaron and I need to get out of here right now. We're coming home and we need bus tickets."

"Whoa, whoa—hold on a second."

I know I'm talking fast, but this is the only way we can get home and I need Uncle Jake to understand. To help us.

"We could stay with you," I say. "Would that be okay?"

Uncle Jake says my name, but I keep talking, right over him.

"I don't even know how much a bus ticket costs."

"Abigail—Abigail." I finally stop, and he says, "Where is your dad?"

My throat gets tight. On the other end of the line, Uncle

Jake sighs. Long and drawn out, like somebody readying themselves for pain.

"I'm not with them anymore."

"Huh? What are you talking about? What happened?"

I hear his voice. I understand the words. But I have no idea where to begin anymore, how to make sense of everything. What happened?—that question no longer applies. Now it's only what's happening. What we will do next. That's all I care about.

"I need to come home," I say.

The line is silent. I hear a truck passing, but I don't know if it's on his end or out on the street. The anger of earlier catches me, sending a crippling exhaustion I've never felt before. I close my eyes and say, "We need your help."

"What does that mean?" he asks. "Where's Aaron?"

I don't answer him and he asks me again, his voice rising.

"I don't know," I say.

His silence says everything.

"I'm going to call that church and straighten your dad's ass out," he finally says. "Right now."

I sit up, because that can't happen. If he calls Dad, then

they'll know what Aaron and I have planned. They'll find us and we'll end up padlocked at Brother John's. It will only be harder to escape the next time.

I don't want to say the next words, but I make myself do it. I'll see him soon enough and can explain. I can apologize then.

"Never mind. It's fine," I say. "I'll see you soon. I love you."

And then I hang up the phone. I sit there in the dark room, the absence of Uncle Jake's voice and my heartbeat the only things I feel.

I hear the voice and jerk awake, not sure where I'm at or what's happening. A man stands above me, holding a vacuum cleaner cord in his hand. "I said: How did you get in here?"

I reach for the backpack I took from Brother John's office, but it's not there. The man holds it out to me. "You get this when you leave the building."

I stand up, and he makes a point of parading me past a group of women in the church's library. They all stare as I pass. I don't look up, moving as fast as my stiff legs will let me.

At the doors of the church, the janitor—the name Merle is stitched into his shirt—hands me my backpack and says, "Next time I'm calling the cops."

I take the bag and walk out into the early morning cold.

Even now, with the streets beginning to fill with people, I am uncomfortable. If anything, the additional bodies make me move even slower. I don't want to walk around a corner and see Skeetch standing there. Or Mom and Dad. So I shuffle through the streets, trying to keep the morning cold from grabbing me.

A dull pain of hunger squeezes my stomach. I could turn around and go back to the church—plead for a meal. But Merle's threat of calling the police feels more real than the emptiness in my gut. And if that happens, it's over. There's no way any cop would let me go without at least a cursory attempt at finding my parents. Not that it probably matters. More than likely, Mom and Dad haven't done a thing to find me. They're probably kneeling in front of the cross right now, dutiful as ever. Praying that I'll magically reappear.

When I come to a McDonald's, I sit on the front step and watch the people pass, wrapping my arms around myself to keep warm. I don't move as people come in and out. Some of them glance at me, but most are intent on keeping their eyes pointed anywhere else. I scan the street. I don't know where else to look for Aaron and Jess besides the park, but I'm not ready to face it yet.

An older lady comes out of the door and hands me a small brown bag. At first, I'm confused. But then I smell the eggs, the sausage. She has a cup of orange juice in her hands. It's almost a rote response when I say, "No thank you."

"Take it," she says. And without another word, sets the bag and the orange juice at my feet and walks away.

I stare at the bag for a second before opening it and pulling out the sandwich. I eat it in three bites and gulp the orange juice down in one long swallow. I could eat five more and still feel hungry.

A manager comes out the door and shoos me off the small staircase, saying I'm not allowed to beg. I don't argue with him or explain that I didn't ask for the food. I put on my backpack and walk slowly toward the park.

I circle the outskirts until I come to the place where everybody usually hangs out. I sneak into the trees and study the hill. I can see E and Silas sitting in a circle with a couple of other guys I don't recognize. Aaron and Jess aren't there.

Something flashes next to me, a glint of light like a quarter at the bottom of a pool. Before I can turn, I hear: "Who will come with me!"

Trumpet Man sits in the bushes, wrapped in a garbage bag. His long blond hair is matted and twisted into what might have once been dreadlocks. His horn, oddly polished considering his clothes and face, sits next to him on top of an overstuffed backpack. He stumbles to his feet and says, "I am bound!"

He trips over his backpack, yelling loudly. I look over to the hill. E is headed toward me, and everybody is watching.

"Please be quiet," I say.

Trumpet Man works his mouth, trying to say something. All that comes out is a loud, "Wide extended plains!" And then, inexplicably, he picks up the trumpet and plays one long note.

I'm about to run away when I hear E's voice.

"Abigail? Is that you?"

Behind me, Trumpet Man is mumbling. E doesn't come into the trees and he speaks low. "What are you doing here?"

"I'm trying to find Aaron and Jess."

At their names, E bends down and pretends to tie his shoe. He looks over his shoulder and then says, "What do you mean, you're trying to find them? Where's your brother?"

"I have no idea," I say. "That's why I'm asking you."

One of the guys yells for E, who waves him off without turning around. "Just stay in the trees. These guys know Skeetch."

I inch closer to the trunk and E says, "So, you haven't been to Sea Cliff?"

"No—what's going on?"

"Oh, shit. Okay, so Jess is there. She got into it with Skeetch last night and then your brother found out and everything went to shit. It's all fucked up, okay?"

Nothing he's saying makes sense. He closes his eyes in an attempt at concentration.

The guys E was sitting with stand up and start walking toward the trees. Behind me, Trumpet Man shifts; the garbage bag he's wearing sounds like dry leaves in the wind. E looks over his shoulder quickly and says, "Aaron was going to the church to find you. So maybe you guys can cross paths. If not, go to Jess. Please."

As I slip out of the trees, I hear E say something about that crazy dude with the trumpet, followed by the unmistakable voice of Trumpet Man: "I am bound!"

I think about going to Sea Cliff, but ultimately it isn't hard to decide which direction to go. I can't let Aaron sit at Brother John's, waiting to be seen by Mom or Dad. By any of the other nameless people we've sat next to night after night. As I walk, I assure myself that he's too smart to be caught. Too smart to let everything get ruined so easily. But when I get to the church, he isn't there. I stand across the street, in the folds of a closed dry cleaner's front porch and watch the block as carefully as I can.

Every time a person appears on the street, I tense—ready to run. Ready to whisper-scream Aaron's name. I imagine his face, shocked—surprised. When he sees me, I'll let him ask his questions—*How? Seriously?*—and then I'll tell him I'm ready to go. That there's nothing holding either of us here anymore.

I'm still thinking about Aaron when the door of the church slams open, hitting the plaster of the building hard enough to dislodge a sizable chunk. And then it's Aaron, looking over his shoulder and running as fast as he can.

I don't think before stepping out into the street and yelling his name. He skids to a stop and stares at me, confused. But he doesn't say anything I expect—*Are you kidding?* or even *What the hell, Abs?* Instead he looks over his shoulder one more time and says, "Run!"

As soon as he says it, Dad comes tearing out of the church—his hair wild with sleep. I don't see Mom, not that I have a chance. Aaron sprints ahead, faster than I thought he could go—I can barely keep up—and we run, quickly outpacing Dad, who yells after us. Both of our names, slowly disappearing among the sound of cars and trains until the only thing I can hear is our feet hitting the ground and our breath, heavy in the cold morning air.

We don't stop until Aaron cuts into the football stadium, going down the steps two at a time until we're both standing on the track. Aaron watches the entrance for any sign of Dad. But even if he was still chasing us, he'd be at least two blocks behind.

"This way," Aaron says, motioning toward a small tunnel where, when the stadium was still in use, the teams would wait before coming onto the field. We catch our breath, neither of us saying anything. I try to erase the picture of Dad, struggling to catch us. His strangled voice. Aaron stands up, hands on top of his head, and stares at me.

"They've probably already called the cops," he says. "You should've waited for me to come back to get you."

I can't bring myself to tell him that Mom and Dad did nothing when he left. They sat in the church, praying—asking God to do something when every moment of the past week should've told them that number was disconnected. And while I'm sure they're worried—Mom is probably sick with it—I know they didn't call the police when they found me gone this morning. The only thing they're doing right now is staring at the ceiling and hoping whatever magic they believe in will still change the world.

"How was I supposed to know you were coming back?"

Aaron lets his hands fall off his head, and he nods. All he says is, "I wouldn't leave you there. You know that."

Aaron doesn't move, except his eyes. They flit around my face, taking in everything. When he speaks, his voice is soft.

"What happened to your head?" I reach up, touching the scrape from last night. We're too close to getting out of here for me to tell him the truth. Who knows what he would do, how he would react.

"Nothing. I fell down when I was running away last night."

He stares at the scrape for a second and then says, "I know you're worried about it, I know you don't want to go—but we need to get out of here today."

At this point, I'd be willing to walk home. Even if it took a year of hiking alongside the highway, stopping to camp wherever we could find a spot.

"I'm ready," I say.

For the first time in my life, I think I might see Aaron cry. Instead he clears his throat and says, "Yeah, well, going back to the church wasn't a total waste." He pulls a small envelope from his pocket and hands it to me. A fat stack of bills is folded inside.

"Where did you get this?"

"Brother John's briefcase. You realize this is the money Mom and Dad gave him, right?"

I nod, because I don't want to think about it. These bills, folded so perfectly into the envelope, are another example of our failure.

Actually, no. Not our failure. Their failure. I need to

retrain my brain, to repurpose the word "we" to only include me and Aaron. I hand the envelope back to him and say, "Is it enough?"

He looks past me, into the heart of the stadium. His face is thin and lined with stress.

"Probably not. But all I care about is getting out of the city," he says. "And we have enough for that. From there, I don't know . . .but I'll figure something out."

"Is Jess okay?"

He says it simply, a flat "No. She's not."

I don't ask what happened, because it doesn't matter. Instead, I imagine us pulling away from the curb in some big bus. Watching as the city grows smaller behind us. We can call Uncle Jake from the bus stop when we reach home. Maybe from wherever we end up. The point is: we're going, and it's better than anything I've felt in months.

"Let's go get her," I say. "Right now."

Aaron stuffs the envelope back into his pocket and shakes his head. "I need you to bring Jess back here. I have to go get the tickets."

"I'll go with you and then we'll get her," I say, because I can't walk away from him again. I don't want to face the city alone anymore.

"I was supposed to get her an hour ago, but then you weren't at the church. . . . I'm trying to keep all the plates in the air, Abs."

I don't know if he means to quote another one of Dad's weird sayings, and he doesn't acknowledge it at all. But when I sigh, he holds out his pinky finger.

This is unchanging. This is omnipotence. The only thing.

I link my pinky finger with his.

This is it. We won't see Mom and Dad again—at least not anytime soon. We'll be gone, like smoke. One more risk and then we're on the bus, the road—whatever it takes. As much as it hurts, I can't deny the excitement of going home.

It feels strangely the same way it did when we first pulled into the city. Dad couldn't stop smiling and butterflies wouldn't leave my stomach. That was how everything started, but when does it end? The end could've been us in North Carolina, at the grocery store, fumbling with government-issued ways of getting food. Every eye on us; being taught how to pay, what to buy, by a kid in my chemistry class. That easily could have been our ending—us, surviving in North Carolina. But it wasn't and I don't know how to act, what to do, except sit there and hold on to Aaron's finger like it's keeping me above water. And maybe if I don't let go, he won't leave. We can go get Jess together.

He pushes my shoulder softly and says, "Hey, it's going to be fine. We're going to get on that bus and everything will be better."

I believe it. More than anything else in my life. I have to.

"Go get Jess," he says. "I'll meet you guys back here in an hour. Maybe two. Stay out of sight, okay?"

"What about you?"

He pulls me into a long hug, whispering in my ear, "It's all good, Abs. We're almost done."

I run to the beach, but can't get comfortable. My legs never loosen and my chest hurts the entire time. When I finally get to the fence, I can hear the ocean and feel the salt on my face as I take the stairs fast. The boulder we shared is empty. Down the small beach, other boulders jut out of the sand, but she's not on any of them.

Still, I run down to the beach and look in every corner I can find. The only people out here are two older men in wetsuits, getting ready to swim out into the foggy bay.

I'm starting to get worried, when to my left something pops out of the ocean. At first, I think it might be a seal or some other kind of animal. Just as quickly, it transforms into sea foam, bubbling and disappearing. Another surge pours into the spot, spraying water high in the air. As it falls, half being carried away by the wind, I see something just beyond the last outcropping of rocks. A small huddled mass, blurred by the creeping fog. It could be a trick of the eyes, rocks and moss blending together—except for the hair. It burns, red as fire.

I lower myself off the boulder and follow the waterline until I'm directly across from her. I have to time the incoming wave, running when it recedes. I gasp as the water flirts with my heels. Jess sits in a small indentation in the rock, wrapped in a sleeping bag. The mini cave would be disguised if she wasn't sitting on its lip. From the beach, this place is almost invisible.

"Don't look at me," she says, turning away. But I can see the damage anyway. Her face is swollen and splashed with cuts. A red line splits her bottom lip, darker than her hair.

She turns back to the bridge, back to the mystery of the water and fog. A place that, at night, looks different—magical. A place you could escape to. But in the daylight it looks normal. Only a bridge.

Neither of us speaks. It's not until the water splashes my foot that I make a sound, a pitiful-sounding squeal.

"It's cold," I say. Jess's eyes glide to my face. She doesn't move, not when the water splashes both of us, or when a strong breeze pushes her hair into her face. She only looks at me. Seeing her face—I can't tear my eyes away—rips into me. The cuts, the dried blood. Did it happen after I saw Skeetch? Did it happen because of me? The idea that he went after Jess because of what I did to him burrows into my brain, slowly dripping into my stomach until I feel sick and can't think of anything else. Between that and the reality of what happened last night, I have to sit down.

"I think this is my fault," I say.

"Fuck that," Jess says. "It's his fault. You didn't do shit."

I don't know who looks away first, but soon we're both staring at the bridge again. The water is slowly crawling toward us and I'm scooting back when Jess sighs and says, "We were together. A while ago. And he thinks that means something."

I try to imagine Jess and Skeetch, but it doesn't compute.

She seems as much a part of Aaron as I am. Connected by something that won't get cut away without a fight.

"Aaron knows some, but not all of it," she continues. "It was when I first got here—I was fourteen. He made me feel special for about a week. Then I was stuck. When he got arrested, I thought it was finished. But, yeah, right."

She looks over at me, and I wish there was something I could say to make her feel better. But everything I come up with—*Sorry*, etc.—feels too weak. For a second, I wonder how Aaron would react. The answer is definitive and comes quick.

"Skeetch is an asshole," I say.

Jess wipes tears out of her eyes. "This is so true."

I want to keep going. To use every word Aaron has ever tried to teach me. Every word I was too scared to use, for fear of what God might think. But is there any other word to describe Skeetch? Fucking asshole, maybe.

But none of the words seem right. None of them are potent enough. So we sit and stare at the bay.

"I ran away." I don't even know why I say it, except that it fills the silence. I don't know when I start crying, but I wipe my eyes. Jess reaches out and puts her hand on my knee, just as another splash of water hits both of us.

"My mom had, like, boyfriends," she says. "I guess I'm the total cliché, because they liked me more than her. And she either didn't care or didn't want to believe it. One day, it just was easier to walk away rather than walk back into that apartment. So, a couple of guys with trucks later and . . ."

She waves her arms in the air.

"What I'm saying is: sometimes you have to leave. Sometimes people don't deserve to have you around."

The water surges forward and soaks the bottom of both our pants. Jess stands up, cursing.

"You know what?" she says. "Screw this city."

She raises both of her middle fingers to the bridge, which sits there oblivious as always. When she reaches her hand down, I take it.

"Get in on this," she says. "It's liberating as hell."

I give the Golden Gate Bridge the finger and so does Jess, both of us standing there until another spray of water jumps from the bay, arcing over our heads and spattering our shirts with foam. And then we run from the water, hand in hand, moving faster than I've ever gone before. Faster than I ever thought was possible.

BEFORE

IT WAS AARON'S IDEA TO GO TO THE PARTY. A GIRL I DIDN'T know—Amber Henson—had invited him. I'd never been to the Deerfield parties, even though they seemed to happen every weekend. I always wanted to know where their parents went, a question that made Aaron roll his eyes. But still. How did they get the beer? Did their parents know? How could they not? The way it got told on the Mondays after, these parties were huge.

Anyway, it was Aaron's idea and we were standing on the steps with at least fifty other people who were yelling and smoking. Everybody had a red cup in their hand.

"Well, this is really fun," I said, but Aaron couldn't hear me because people started screaming even louder. Or he was ignoring me. That was possible, too.

"Did you see that? I think that girl just hit that guy," he said. He was pointing in the door, but I couldn't see anything except the ocean of heads that multiplied in front of me infinitely.

And then he disappeared into the crowd, as if he'd jumped into a pool of deep water. He was there, and then he wasn't.

I tried to push my way through, but by the time I made it into the living room I couldn't see him anywhere. Whatever had happened in the living room was over, but people were still laughing and pointing out another door. A huge window opened to the back, where a pool lit the yard an electric blue. I assumed Aaron had somehow made his way out there, because it seemed like our entire school was circling that pool. I worked my way through the crowd until somebody grabbed me by my elbow and said, "Is your brother here?"

Aaron was the outgoing one, the one who had friends I'd never even spoken to. People who represented nearly every category in the school, a trick I always wished I could master. But this girl, holding one of those same red cups, was someone I knew.

Chelsea Taylor had liked Aaron since we were in sixth grade, but I think she scared him more than he would admit. She was pretty and knew it. The sort of girl who had a new boyfriend every month.

"He's here somewhere," I said.

Before I could finish talking, she let out this little squeal and raised her cup high above her head, sloshing clear liquid over the side. It fell into her hair, but she didn't seem to care. "I love your brother. He's so funny. Do you remember that thing he said one time at the assembly?"

I gaped at her, clueless. Not that it mattered. She sighed and said, "He's so great. But you know that because you're his sister."

And then she laughed, crazily.

"I'll tell him you said hi," I said, but she seemed unaware that I had spoken. She looked to the ceiling, as if she was trying to remember the answer to a question, and let out a long, emphatic "Wooo!"

I threaded my way through the rest of the crowd and finally found Aaron sitting next to the pool with a group of his friends. They were laughing, but stopped as soon as I walked up. Aaron said, "What's up, Abs?"

"Besides you ditching me? Nothing," I say. "Oh, and Chelsea Taylor says hello."

He went red and his friends started saying things like "Uh-oh, A-Team! and "Somebody's about to get lucky!," which turned me red, too. I still was able to force out, "And I want to leave."

"Leave?" It came from a collection of voices and, almost immediately, Aaron's friend Mike pulled a chair into their circle and said, "A-Team, part deux! Sit down and drink a beer."

Aaron tried to hide his cup, his face. But I made it a point to stare at both.

"Especially now that the world is ending," Mike said, laughing.

"C'mon, man," Aaron said. "Lay off."

"What? I'm just having fun. Chill the hell out."

"Don't tell me to chill out. You're the one acting like an asshole."

Mike's eyes went big with surprise and he said, "Oh, I'm the asshole? Good to know." He took a drink from his beer and then said, "But at least my dad isn't some crazy fundamentalist. The sky is falling! The sky is falling!"

Aaron hit him hard, right on the nose. Mike fell back

in his chair, blood streaming down his face, onto his shirt. Shane, one of Aaron's other friends, grabbed him before he could punch Mike again.

"What the hell, Aaron?"

But Aaron was gone, back into the guts of the house. When I finally found him, he was sitting next to the mailbox by the road. People passed, but nobody looked at either of us as I sat down next to him and said, "Are you okay?"

He looked up into the night sky, the stars. Behind us, the party continued generating noise. I swear I could even hear Chelsea's "Wooo!" calling out to us like a beacon from somewhere deep inside the house.

FIFTEEN

WE WALK BACK TOWARD THE STADIUM SLOWLY. THE BRAVADO OF the beach is gone, and Jess pauses at every voice that rises up above the bustle. We both stop when the park comes into view.

"It will take forever to go around," Jess says. "We have to go through."

Still, we don't move. The light changes three times before I say, "Can you run?"

Jess nods, and when the light turns green, we jog across the road and down into the park. I expect to lead us through, to go slow so she can keep up. But as soon as we hit the grassy middle she takes off, quickly putting ten feet between us. And no matter how fast I push myself, I can't make up the distance.

Jess stops next to the playground, bending over like she's going to puke. We're so close to the entrance, we can walk the rest. When my name rings out over the noise of the park, I'm initially confused. It's familiar and at first I want to smile—to run toward it. But when I turn and see Mom standing there, looking scared and anxious, my stomach drops into my knees.

I go to run and Mom says, "Abigail, wait!"

She doesn't move toward me, but every muscle in my body is tense, like the moments before a race—ready to move, to react. Mom holds out her hands, like I'm standing on the edge of a cliff.

"I just want to talk," she says.

I can't look at her. Not at her dirty jeans or her shirt, equally stained. She looks exactly like every other homeless person in this park. So do I. And if anybody were to walk up on her right now, they'd think, Oh great, another one.

"I don't want to talk," I say.

Her voice is quiet, barely audible as she says, "Okay. I understand that. But maybe five minutes? We can take a walk around the park."

"Is Dad here?"

She blinks once, twice, before saying, "No, honey. He's not."

Jess comes up next to me and says, "Is everything okay?"

Mom looks at me for the answer.

"It's fine," I say. "I'll be back in a second."

Jess nods, not looking at Mom. I wait until she's back in the trees before I turn to Mom and say, "Okay."

The park feels the way our house would when I would stay home sick. Lit differently. As if somebody turned up the volume on everything whenever we went to school. And while that was exciting, this is torture. Mom barely looks at me as we walk the asphalt trails.

Trumpet Man is near the entrance, playing loudly.

I try to conjure the anger I had in Brother John's office, because if both of us disappearing won't wake them up, then nothing will. They're stuck asking the same questions and looking for the same answers.

I don't want to listen to her explain about how God is going to help us.

Finally Mom turns to me, her face so expectant. It's the way Dad looks whenever Brother John stands up in front of us. As if I can unravel a problem so dried and twisted by simply opening my mouth. But words will only tie the knot of our problems tighter. So I don't say anything. I don't ask where Dad is, because I already know the answer. All that matters is he isn't here.

It takes a long time for her to speak. When she does, her voice is soft.

"I don't want to be here, either."

I look at her and she smiles.

"Really. Why would I want to leave everything behind? But there are some things you do because you know it's true, and other things you do because you have faith."

Here we go.

"And what if you don't have faith anymore?" I ask, ready for a fight. She turns and stares at a group of kids playing soccer.

"Then you have faith in the things you know will never let you down," she says. "Your dad's trying his best."

It makes my skin crawl, and whatever is left of my old inhibition disappears.

"His best? Dad hasn't done anything since we came to this city," I say. Before she can tell me that we're being watched over, that God will provide and is in control, no matter what—before she can tell me any of it for the thousandth time—I say, "I'm leaving, Mom. Aaron, too. I can't do this anymore."

Her face shrinks. She opens her mouth. But I'm too fast again.

"It's not okay," I say, turning away from her. "Don't say that."

The cold of the afternoon crystallizes my breath. Everything in the park moves, except us.

For a few seconds, she lets me stand there, ignoring her. Then she reaches out and fixes my hair, tucking it behind my ears and trying to tame it with her palms. When it looks good, or she's given up, she says, "Is your brother okay?"

A million things fly through my head. Jess and Aaron and how they act when they're together. How I'm not sure, even if some miracle did occur, Dad and Mom would welcome some street girl into our lives. The tiny voice saying Aaron has been right all along is louder than anything else and I want to lash out at her, to ask why she cares now. But her eyes are big and her face is creased with worry.

I let my head drop and I take a deep breath.

"Well, you just met his girlfriend," I say. "Jess."

If this surprises her, she doesn't show it.

"She's coming with us," I say.

When I look at Mom, she's still composed and it bothers me. Why isn't she reacting? Why isn't she trying to pull me back to the church? Does she not care at all? Something jumps inside me, and I don't know what to feel. Whether I should be relieved or angry. Behind her, Jess appears from inside the trees. She doesn't come closer, respectful of whatever she assumes is happening between me and Mom. But she points at her wrist and I nod.

I expect Mom to ask me to come with her—to remind me that God will help us, just like everything and anything else. That if we bend our knees and lift up our words, everything about our life will pop back into place. All of it tied together with a pretty bow.

But she doesn't.

She says, "How are you getting home?"

It makes me stumble. I don't know if I should tell her, if this is some kind of trap. But then she takes my hand and says, "I don't know what to do anymore, Abigail. But I need to know that you and your brother are going to be okay. So tell me how you and Aaron are getting home, so at least I have that much."

Hearing it—seeing her so broken—tears something deep inside me. The place where I always thought God lived—soul level. But maybe it's not so clearly separated. Maybe our love and our faith are intertwined in one messy ball, unable to be distinguished from each other as easily as we'd like.

Mom smiles, still sad, and shakes her head. It's only then that I realize she's the one saying good-bye to me.

"We're taking the bus," I say.

"Okay," she says. "You should call your Uncle Jake. He'll let you stay with him. That way, you won't be . . ."

She doesn't finish, instead hugging me so hard I can barely breathe. "I love you and your brother more than anything," she says. "Don't forget that, okay?"

When she lets me go, we're both wiping our eyes. In that moment, I'd go with her anywhere she asked. "About the money your brother took," she says.

I drop my head, ready for the admonishment—but also to tell her that we're not giving any of it back. She lifts my head up with her hand and smiles.

"Keep it," she says. "How many billboards does one man need? I mean, seriously."

There's this moment, right before we get tangled up in

laughter, when she reaches down and squeezes my hand.

When the laughter stops, while we're still staring at each other, Mom says, "I need to get back to the church. Your father will be wondering what happened to me."

"Come with us," I say. I have no idea how much money's in the envelope, if it would be enough for all of us to make it back to North Carolina. But it would be close. And I'm still willing to take that kind of chance.

Mom looks down. "Honey, I need to be here for your father. Regardless of how you feel right now, he's a good person. He really is. And besides, you and Aaron have always had each other. Guardian angels, the both of you. This is all going to work out. I promise it will."

When she steps back, I don't cry. I stand there waiting for her to walk away—the strangest thing I've ever felt. She wipes the tears away from her cheek and says, "Tell your brother I love him. Okay? And when you get home, call me at the church."

SIXTEEN

I'M STILL TRYING TO STEADY MYSELF WHEN JESS WALKS UP.

"Was that your mom?"

"Yeah," I say.

"Oh, wow. Are you okay?"

That has always been the question, and my answer waffles with each step we take out of the park. Half of me wants to run to Aaron and tell him exactly what she said, every word, so he can have one good memory of her. But I also want to know why she isn't fighting for us. Why she's pushing us to the interstate when the other option—her staying with us, no matter what—is so much easier.

Will we go without her? Yes. There is no doubt.

We'll get on that bus and follow a slow and crooked

map across the country, drawing closer to home every single day. We'll smell the pine trees and Uncle Jake will meet us at the bus stop downtown, instantly trumping all of our problems. We won't have to wait for anything, except maybe the bathroom—Uncle Jake's house isn't that big—but what does that matter? After months of endings, I'm ready for a beginning. And if it has to be without Mom and Dad, so be it. We will start over. We will live.

As Jess and I walk through the park, people move in a hundred different directions. One catches a Frisbee as another bends over with belly laughter. A woman sits alone on a bench, a newspaper folded like a fan in front of her face. Behind the trees, a siren blares as it tears down the street. Soon, another follows. Then a third. Birds come from the trees in a flourish, blacking out the sky for a second before dissolving into hundreds of similar shapes that dart in every direction. In the center of everything Trumpet Man is lying beside a huge tree, softly playing his horn.

"Take one more look," I say to Jess, glancing around the park. "Because North Carolina is not this exciting."

Jess puts a hand on my shoulder and says, "I'm so ready for boring. Trust me."

I start to laugh, but Jess jumps back so quickly she trips on my foot and falls to the ground, hard. Before I know what's happening, she's up—staring at Skeetch standing on the path with his arms stretched out. Like he wants a hug. The two guys I saw with E flank either side of him, one short with a Mohawk. The other, seemingly too young to sport the giant skull tattoo that dominates his forearm.

I step in front of Jess and say, "If you come any closer, I'll scream."

Skeetch doesn't react, only looks over my shoulder at Jess and smiles. "Yeah? They'll probably send the army and the navy to help."

The two boys titter behind him, their faces worked into amused smirks. I step toward them, even though I can't stop my legs from shaking. My hands are fists and when Skeetch sees them, he and his friends nearly collapse in laughter.

"Damn, look at you being all feisty. I like it."

The guy with the tattoo says, "Oh yeah, hurt me. Please."

"You do need to be careful with Little Sister here," Skeetch says, grabbing his crotch. "She really doesn't play nice."

"Just leave us alone," Jess says from behind me, her voice barely audible over the noise from the park. As she says it, the Mohawk parrots it back to her—"Leave us alone! Leave us alone!" The three of them laugh even harder.

I look around for a police officer, for Aaron or even E—anybody paying attention. But despite all the people, I've never felt so alone.

When Skeetch takes a step forward, I hate that I flinch. He smiles and says, "Why all the drama? Nobody's trying to start something. If you want to go, then go."

He steps to the edge of the path with a flourish, sweeping his arms to the side as if he were ushering us into a dance. "Go on. Nobody's stopping you."

Without a second thought, I grab Jess's arm and pull her between them, ignoring their eyes, their smell. Everything about them. At the last second, Skeetch grabs the back of my shirt and pulls me against his body, pinning my arms to my hips. His mouth is close to my ear.

"When you see your brother, tell him I said hello, okay?"

And then he lets me go and the three of them cackle with laughter as they disappear into the park.

"Are you okay?" I ask Jess. She nods, and that's all I need to start moving.

The football field is a half-mile away, but I swear it only takes seconds for us to get there. I walk fast, trying not to look over my shoulder. Trying not to worry about Skeetch and his friends.

All I want to do is get to the stadium, find Aaron, and leave.

Above us, the clouds are still rolling in off the mountains, turning the whole world gray. As we come through the arched entrance, I do a quick scan of the stadium. The track is empty, as is the grassy field. In the far corner of the bleachers, I think I see somebody lying down, but as we get closer it turns out to be a forgotten towel.

"He's probably in the tunnel," I say, pointing to the far side. But it's locked, chained so securely that I second-guess whether we actually stood there just a few hours ago.

Jess points to the top of the bleachers and says, "Look."

A large press box frames the center of the stadium. Behind that, a side street runs parallel, at even level with the top row of bleachers. It takes a second for me to realize the entire stadium is built into the side of a hill. We're effectively in a giant hole.

I take the bleacher steps two at a time. When I get to the top, I look out onto the street. A couple is walking a small white dog with their daughter, but I don't see Aaron anywhere. I come back to the lip of the stadium just as Jess is reaching the top.

"Do you guys have a special spot in here? Something I wouldn't know about?"

Because he should be here. Even if the bus station was on the other side of town, there's no way we beat him back to the stadium. Not after the trip back from Sea Cliff and talking to Mom.

"No," Jess says. "I don't think we ever came here together."

As she's talking, my eyes settle on a small patch of grass separated from the road by the same iron gate that circles the stadium. From here, all I can see is empty fast food bags and a couple of open beer cans rolling across the hard cement.

But then something moves in the shadow of the press box and I hear my name. At first I smile, but the closer I get, the more I can see. Aaron's trying to stand up, leaning all of his body weight against a cement retaining wall, clutching his stomach.

I run to him and he falls back to the grass.

His face is broken. There are cuts and bruises and his nose is bent sideways. One eye focuses on me while the other, blood red and beginning to swell, stares vacantly over my shoulder. He tries to sit up, but a painful gurgling sound brings him back to the grass.

"Oh my God," I say. Behind me, Jess starts screaming. She runs forward and tries to grab Aaron. As soon as she touches him, he winces.

"Go call an ambulance," I tell her. "Now."

"No hospital," Aaron says. "They'll call Mom and Dad."

Jess hesitates. "He needs an ambulance," I say. "Go!"

She runs out of the stadium, yelling for a cell phone and harassing each person she sees until she's got one in her hand. Aaron gasps her name out, and I put my hand on his shoulder.

"She's going to get help. Just rest, okay?"

"Get her out of here. Before they come back."

I can barely understand him. Every word is drowning, choked. When he tries to sit up again, his voice is pained. "Please. Go."

I try to guide him back down to the grass as gently as

I can. He fights me with every bit of energy he has left, which can't be much because it's only a few seconds before he's back on the grass, his chest tightening with every awkward breath. Every time I look at his face, I have to blink back tears. I want to believe that we're still going. That it's just a matter of Aaron getting patched up and then we can get on a bus. We have to hit pause, for only a second.

He tries to say something, and I lean closer so that I can hear.

"They took the money. I'm sorry, Abs."

Jess comes running back to us. She kneels down next to him, holding his head in her hands. I watch her cry over Aaron, her hair falling into his face as she does it. In the distance sirens begin calling. As soon as he hears them, Aaron starts mumbling—trying to push himself off the ground in a panic.

"They'll call . . . can't. Please."

When the paramedics arrive, they push us aside. One paramedic gives Aaron a shot while the other asks me and Jess all kinds of questions that I either don't know or don't want to answer. How it happened. His blood type. If he's allergic to any medicine. The last question is the worst.

"Does he have parents? Any family?"

I watch as they stabilize his neck in a large yellow brace. I don't know if I should tell them about Mom and Dad, or even if I should let them put him in the ambulance. I know he's hurt, but what happens if they bring us back?

"Hey—does he have any family?"

"He's a street kid," the other paramedic says. "Let's not worry about family."

I hear the words and the anger climbs through my body. A small group of people collect on the sidewalk, watching the paramedics work, snapping pictures with their cell phones. When Aaron gets to the hospital, the staff will eventually track down Mom and Dad. They'll figure out that he's not just another street kid and then—what? All of this starts over?

The first paramedic pops the stretcher up, until Aaron is lying at waist level. His eyes are closed, the drugs taking effect.

Seeing him like that makes me want to unhook all the tubes and machines from his body, and carry him away—to do this on our own, the way we've been planning. And I hate the impulse. There should be no question whether Aaron should be in the ambulance. We shouldn't have to worry if social services will swoop in, or if we'll even be able to pay for this ride to the hospital.

But of course, that is the problem. And has been for too long.

And maybe Mom wants us to go. Maybe that makes her feel better, knowing that we aren't stuck here going to service after service.

But I want them to know what we had to do to get away. The last thing we had to give up for God, for Brother John. I want them to look me in the eye and say that we aren't more important than whatever is going to fall out of the sky.

I nudge Jess forward slightly. "Wait, this is his sister."

She looks at me, shocked, but I push her forward again and say, "He needs you to stay with him."

The paramedic looks at us skeptically, but then tells her to follow him to the truck. Just before they pull away, I run up to the side and ask where they're taking him.

And then I turn around and run straight back to Brother John's.

SEVENTEEN

I STORM INTO THE CHURCH, NEARLY KNOCKING OVER THE CROSS trying to get at Mom and Dad. Brother John's mouth drops when I step right in front of Dad and say, "Aaron's hurt."

"Brother Dale, I will not have this—not now."

Dad looks at his palms and, maybe for the first time, I agree with Brother John—not now. He can't disappear now, not when Aaron is riding across town in an ambulance. Not now.

Brother John tries to lead me away from the front of the room and I push him away. Anger takes control of my lips. My voice could shake the windows.

"He's in an ambulance right now." I show him the

blood on my hands. On my jeans, which now are really ruined.

Mom says, "Abigail, what happened?"

"Who here believes in God's plan?" Brother John addresses the group, his voice tight. Booming across the small room.

A few hands initially shoot into the air, but drop when Mom spins around and stabs the air with her finger. If it were a weapon, Brother John wouldn't be standing.

"Don't," she says.

Dad comes to her and wraps his arms around her shoulders, trying to whisper in her ear. She shrugs him off. Her body is rigid, yet every so often little tremors ripple across her skin. When he tries again she says, "Dale, no. Do you hear me? No."

"We need to go right now, Mom."

Mom turns to face Dad, her face hard. "I'm leaving, Dale. And you need to decide if you're coming with us."

Dad looks at Mom, and then my hands.

"We need some intervention for this family, Lord." Brother John prays with his eyes closed. Only a few people in the room join him. "Help them see the Deceiver clearly and know that only through you can we find happiness."

I turn to Dad and say, “God doesn’t need you here, Dad. But Aaron does. Please.”

“Are you sure?”

Dad says it plainly, like I’m trying to sell him a car. It shocks me, even though I’ve heard the same refrain a hundred times. I stare at him with my mouth open.

Maybe it can be just me, Aaron, and Mom. Jess. We’ll leave Dad here to wait with Brother John. But we’ll go, and if he ever decides to join us, then fine. But I don’t need him to be onboard. Not anymore.

But instead of seeing the Dad I have come to expect—stupidly faithful and ready to mortgage what little we have left—he takes my hand and holds it tight, like I might blow away.

Dad says it again. “Are you sure?”

“Dad . . .”

He hesitates, and then says, “I wasn’t talking to you, Abigail.”

When he looks up, his jaw is set. His eyes are focused on Brother John, still praying at the front of the room. “Brother John,” Dad says. “I need to know if you’re sure.”

Brother John doesn’t hesitate.

“God asks us to cut away the withered branches in our

lives. That's what I know. Like it's my own name, Brother Dale. And if you don't?" He laughs here, spiteful and loud. "Well, then maybe your eternal destination isn't as clear as I once thought."

Dad nods and my heart drops into my stomach. "This is my son, Brother John. I need more than that."

Brother John spins around to face me, grabbing my shoulders hard enough to make me cry out. "You are willing to lead your entire family astray? You're willing to live with the eternal consequences of your idolatry and childishness? You—"

Dad pulls Brother John away from me, separating us with his body. Despite the tears that crowd his eyes and cheeks, he looks strong. Almost scary. Brother John stands there, rubbing his hands together and staring past Dad to me.

"You want a sign, Brother Dale? After everything you've been through, you have the audacity to ask God to give you another sign? Go ahead and leave, but God isn't going to let you come back in."

Quickly—before I know it's happening—Aaron's face flashes into my head. It's like he's filling me with bravado, taking control of my body, because I take a step, then two, hoping Mom and Dad will follow me. That I've read the situation correctly. And as I begin to leave the room I say, "We'll take our chances."

Dad reaches his hand for me to take as Brother John addresses the crowd, saying, "Go ahead and leave. Walk away from the only thing that will ever give meaning to your life. Because that reward in Heaven's going to be sweet, yes sir. Can I get an *amen*?"

I try to think of something to say as we walk to the back of the church. Something clever. Something with teeth. But when I open the door, holding it for Mom and Dad, I realize I don't have to say anything. Everything that needs to be said is happening right now as we walk through this door.

NOW

I COME ACROSS A LITTLE CHAPEL IN THE BASEMENT OF THE hospital. It's dark and everything seems to be covered in red—the carpet, the cushions. Even the small Bibles that dot the back of each pew look like blood. An older woman is playing the piano, singing loudly from the hymnal even though the chapel is empty.

I am bound.

I am bound.

I am bound for the promised land.

I smile. The only thing missing is a trumpet solo.

It could be a sign. It could be a message. I don't know. But after the initial pause of recognition, I start walking again, following the cramped hallways of the hospital.

I'm trying to feel comfortable inside again, even though it's strange when I get too warm and have to pull off my sweatshirt.

Aaron's room is full of machines and people. Mom, Dad, Jess—Uncle Jake will be here tomorrow. The doctors say Aaron will be okay, and every time they say it I let myself smile. Because even though I know they mean physically, that his cuts will heal and the bruises will eventually disappear—I can finally believe it.

We are okay.

ACKNOWLEDGMENTS

There's a reason why people thank agents and editors before God, country, and all manner of family. They walk the road with you. Michael Bourret is the type of agent you want on such a journey. Tireless and smart and awesome. Thank you, sir.

My book was like those kids who go on daytime television to get yelled at by a drill sergeant. Martha Mihalick whipped it—and me—into shape. Eternal gratitude for seeing what I could not.

Molly O'Neill has always been an energetic supporter of my writing and this book. She may not be my editor, but I'm happy to call her a friend.

Speaking of friends, I've got a ton. Thanks to Nova Ren Suma, Ray Veen, Mike Martin, Suzanne Young, Lisa Schroeder, Chris Hoke, Laura Turner, Callie Feyen, Chris Warner, Chrysta Brown—I'm leaving out so many—Jill Reid, Jacob Buckenmeyer, Mike Jung, Alison Clement, Kristin Starnes, and Heidi Weisel. Every one of you is important to me, and I can't imagine having done this without your friendship and support.

Steve Brezenoff, Jeff Geiger. Let's go to NYC again soon.

Aaron Guest, Matt Slye, Paul Luikart, Seth Riley: Great writers. Brothers. Cobras.

Thanks to Greg Wolfe, who directs the MFA program at Seattle Pacific University, and to both Robert Clark and Gina Ochsner, mentors in the truest sense of the word.

My family allows me to disappear for hours on end, and for that I'm eternally grateful. Thanks to my mom, Barb Skelley, who has shown undying and constant support of my writing. My kids, Nora and Ben, would probably prefer I wrote books about dragons and wizards, but as they once said, "Your books are okay too." Listen, I'll take it. And finally, thanks to my wife, Michelle, who deals with the manic brunt of my writing life. High, low, meh—she's there and I can't thank her enough.